real food

real fast

Sam Stern

and Susan Stern, who got him started

WALKER BOOKS
AND SUBSIDIARIES
LONDON · BOSTON · SYDNEY · AUCKLAND

contents

introduction

Hi. I'm Sam Stern. And I'm passionate about my cooking. But that's no big secret. Since **Cooking Up A Storm** came out everyone knows what I've been up to. That book put together all our old-style family recipes. **Real Food, Real Fast**'s a bit different. Like me I guess.

I'm loads taller. (Sorry Dad. Way it goes.) There's been a ton of school work to do, exams, coursework deadlines, etc. Low point? Our cat walked out and didn't come back. High spots? I scored a good few goals at footie. Really got into my cricket. Was well honoured to meet food hero Jamie Oliver (legend). Antony Worral Thompson got me carving up a skinny pheasant in front of a live audience (no pressure there then). I found myself half-asleep on the old BBC breakfast sofa (a real rollercoaster that one) talking teen life, food and how cooking for yourself can make you independent. Hey, you get the picture. But I've still found ways to keep up my cooking.

How? Sundays I do the Sunday Challenge. I give myself half a day to cook new stuff. Three courses. No time limits. Whatever else is going down I get in there and just do it. Brilliant. The rest of the week I make the most of what I've got time-wise and foodwise. Which is where this book comes in. **Real Food, Real Fast** is all about time and how to fit great cooking and real eating into your speedy lifestyle.

It's pretty obvious the way the book's organized. There's a system. Each coloured time-tag section (5 minutes, 10, 15, 20, 30) has recipes that usually take me that time to prep and cook. But hey, don't panic if it takes you longer. Cooking's not an exact science. You get distracted, a call on your mobile, your oven plays up, you're in a dopey sort of mood, you lose the spice, the plot, you're new to cooking (remember I've been doing it since I was 3), it's not a problem. Don't beat yourself up. It's not an exam. Time's just a ballpark figure sort of guide. You cook something a few times and inevitably you're gonna get faster.

And it's all good. Here's the crack – fast food doesn't have to be junk food. Take pizzas – they're great if made with the real stuff and fresh at home using my olive oil style dough, great bubbly tomato garlic topping, fresh herbs, olives and cheeses. Beats anything in a box to my thinking. And I'm lovin' kebabs and kievs made the home-style way. You can't get better than my proper burger. You'll find all these fast foods in here and more. Tex-Mex, soufflés, chocolate pud, risottos, fruit, steak, stir-fry, tortillas, curries, smoothies, soups, mash, salads and veg. Tell you, when you can DIY it this fast and this good you don't need ready-made food made from rubbish ingredients.

Which brings us to shopping. Do it. It's the first step for real home cooking. To help you out I've listed the main ingredients I reckon you'll need. Stuff for your cupboard, fridge, freezer. Food shopping's a really cool thing to do. I'm lucky enough to live in a town that's got a couple of good delis, a great butcher who'll recommend stuff and tell you how to cook it, a daily market with a fish stall, and weekends we get the farmers' market.

These people know the real stuff so talk to them like I do. Pick up all the tips you can. Drop in on the way back from school, whenever. Get in touch with your food. Check out that it's real. Don't get ripped off. Smell it. Touch it. Poke your chicken. It should be firm not spongy and springy. Check it's not been pumped with water and whatever. You want your chemicals in the lab not your dinner. Check out good cheeses, fresh fruit and veg, the right pastas, rice and grains for the job. Everything from your salt and pepper through to your bread (try doing your own). Cooking oils make a lot of difference to the final taste (never mind what they do to you). I'm not dissing supermarkets by the way. There are foods there that you won't easily find anywhere else. We all use them. Just spread your shopping.

The other great strategy is cooking ahead. Back in the dark ages when my mum learned to cook at school (bring back cooking in schools) it was called réchauffé cooking (reheating). Now we call it leftovers, which sounds a bit more basic but it's still brilliant. Do it. Here's how it works. When you're cooking something like my cheat's bolognese to go with spag, you make twice as much. Then you've got a great sauce to, say, stuff and bake with rice in peppers, or stick it into my poppy seed crêpes for a great snack. Or top with my lovely-jubbly creamy mash for a great little cottage pie and bake next day.

Fridging stuff you've got left-over is a great little time trick (you'll find a load of time tricks round here). Have a look at the five minute section. There in all its wonder is my roast chicken alongside a honey roast gammon, roast beef, a chicken liver paté. Obviously they didn't cook in five minutes. But if you've got them in the fridge and you've got all your other bits of shopping in (good bread, fruit and veg, your pickles, etc.) it'll only take you five to decide what to put with it, to slice it and plate it!

Get to the 15 minute section and you'll find I've set you a time challenge. Getting everything on the plate at the same time's a real skill. Some adults I know can't do it. Maybe that's why they rely on prepacked meals where every bit of the job's done for

you. (How boring and disgusting's that?) All you've got to do is sort out an order for doing stuff. The cooking times are set out in the methods. Take your pick – main – sauce – veg – salad – dressing. Bit of mental maths. How hard's that? It's not. When I'm doing a load of stuff and I'm working in a hurry I'll get a pencil and write myself a timetable on my oven.

So you've got a really cool system here that'll set you up with a real-life way to cook. It'll sort you out for when you're home alone doing it for yourself. For when you've got mates round. For impressing a girl, or two … OK, three or four (?!). Exams looming? (Every blueberry helps.) Into a training regime and important matches coming up? Going trekking for a couple of days? Gran round or parents in late? Sorted. Then there's food for the best times – mates heading round for a party. Music on and get yourself cooking.

time trick top ten

Don't let time panic you. Just get on and use it. Make the kitchen your space. Get a sous-chef if you want or clear everyone out and put your music on. It's your time for cooking so damn well enjoy it.

1 Don't waste time wandering round your kitchen looking for an ingredient or piece of equipment. Get organized so you can make the most of it.

2 Veg chopped small takes a shorter time to cook – yeah, yeah, I know it's obvious…

3 Need the oven? Switch it on, get it hot, first thing you do.

6 Use time well. If you're waiting about for something to boil or marinate, use it to prep something else, e.g. blitz a juice or dress a salad.

4 Save time and energy by using the right sized pan. (Suits you. Suits the planet.)

5 Water can take ages to boil so try not to use too much. Get that lid on the pan for speedier heating.

7 Extra time suits food like curries, bolognese, marinating meat, so why not do 'em the day before and fridge 'em.

8 Make more food than you need at a time. Double soup. More spuds. More pizza bases. That's loadsa time saved and other meals sorted.

9 Take opportunities. If you've got bread left-over, blitz for crumbs, stick it in the freezer for when you need it. Make stock from roast. Freeze fruit for crumbles, yogurt bowls and smoothies.

10 Speed up with the right stuff. A sharp knife's faster than a blunt one. Try a hand blender. Get accurate scales and a sharp grater.

Relax, you've got 5 minutes

So, not the time to be sorting an eight-course meal for you, your mates and the dog, then. But time enough on the clock to go for my great combos. It's a pretty neat system and you win. You get to eat some exquisite tastes. It's real. It sorts you out (mood, appetite, focus, training, partying, etc.). It doesn't involve cooking at this point (the trick is to create stuff the day or weekend before when you've time to chill).

So, OK, it needs shopping, but that's easy enough to sort. Our best deli's over the road from the coolest clothes shop and next to the skate place. And top trumps, it's not a cheat. Sorting taste combos is one of the great skills for seriously good cooking.

Brisk breads & speedy extras

Bread – I'm lovin' it. I'd say it's too cool for school but I'd be lying. I take it in most days. In sarnies. On its own. At home bread's always top part of a 5-minute combo. Quick snack or part of a plate? Find a great baker or try Mum's famous treacle bread (lasts a week). The great classic white or my fast scone bread.

Combo
Good bread – focaccia, ciabatta or good crusty white (page 124)
Plate of olives – your choice
Good glug of extra virgin olive oil

Bread, olive oil & olives for nibbling & dipping

I like to use focaccia, ciabatta or my white for this dip. Olive oil's good for you and tastes brilliant. Buy it small and see which you like. (I like it fruity.) Read the labels or ask at the deli. Olives also come in many guises. Marinated in herbs, chillis, pitted, green, black, big and small. Ask to taste in the deli – they'll sort you. This is a great combo and cool ritual. Top snack. Prep time – 1 minute?

Method
1. Tear or slice bread.
2. Pour oil onto dipping plate.
3. Slap your olives on the side.
4. Dip bread into oil. Impressive.

Combo
Slice of bread
Dollop of chicken liver pâté
Chutney
Dill pickle
Baby pickled onions
1 crisp apple (Cox or English favourite)

Bread, chicken liver pâté, pickles, chutney, apple

I like treacle bread (page 125) with this one, but a crusty white or wholemeal works. Track down the pâté (page 124) or get a good deli one. Team with a great chutney. Try my apple (page 124). Mates love this. Impress the girlfriend.

Method

1. Slap bread on plate (no need for butter).
2. Add slice of pâté, chutneys and pickles.
3. Wash and slice your apple. Go eat.

Bread, deli meats, tomato, pickles

Deli meats need character bread. Try your Italian ciabatta, focaccia and your own. Buying stuff in the deli can be intimidating. Hey, don't lose your cool. Ask for a few slices of Parma or Serrano ham. Smoked chicken and turkey work. Point at any salami or another random meat. Try it. You might like it.

Method

1. Spread bread with a little butter or put a little olive oil on plate.
2. Spread deli meat out carefully in single layer. (Thin cured hams can rip.)
3. Cut tomato in quarters. Add pickles. Enjoy yourself.

Combo
Slice of great bread
Little butter or olive oil
Few slices of deli meat
1 Good ripe tomato
Any pickles

Bread, cheese, deli meats, pickles

If you've got a brown and a white bread in, get a slice of both. Thing with combos is to keep changing tastes and textures, like sticking some good cheese in there with the meat. Which go together? Find out. Hang round the cheese counter in your deli. They'll give you free tastes. (Cool – that's lunch sorted.)

Method

1. Butter bread.
2. Slice cheese. Layer meat up.
3. Slap on the chutney.

Combo
Slices of white and
  brown bread
Bit of butter (unsalted's
  sweeter)
Deli meat of choice
Cheeses – try a mix of:
  Wensleydale (crumbly)
  Cheddar (hard)
  Lancashire (tart)
  Vignotte (softer)
  Brie (very soft)
  Stilton (blue and bitey)
My apple chutney (page
  124)

Speedy Med stuff

The taste of holidays all year round. Yes! Mozzarella's magnificent. Parma ham's a brilliant speedy eat. It's lean and it's subtle. Get good stuff from the deli or supermarkets. Vacuum-packed, it's got a massive sell-by date so it'll be there for when you've got 5.

Combo
Parma ham
Mozzarella
1 ripe tomato
1 shallot, sliced
Few bits of rocket or
    other green leaf
Balsamic dressing

Parma ham & mozzarella plate

Possibly my all-time favourite fast plate. Mozzarella comes in handy packs which also have a long shelf-life. Get it in the ball shapes. I eat this for lunch, late-night snack, post-school snack, breakfast. Keep a dressing in the fridge to spark up your combos.

Method
1. Lay ham on plate.
2. Slice mozzarella and tomato. Arrange in single layer.
3. Scatter shallot over tomato. Tip rocket on plate.
4. Drizzle dressing (page 122) over rocket and mozzarella.

Combo
Parma ham
Ripe melon

Ham & melon

Melon gives you loads of energy but it's a good fit eat. Test-drive when you're buying. Press the flesh. It should give a bit. Sniff. It should smell sweet. Works with the slightly salty quality of the Parma.

Method
1. Cut twice into melon from top to toe with a sharp knife.
2. Pull out the slice. Chuck seeds away. Slice off skin. Lay on plate.
3. Add Parma ham. It's that simple.

Rapid roasts

As time-tricks go, this one's king. Cook up a great roast (p 120–1). Eat lovely and hot with trimmings. When it's cold, slap it in the fridge. There it is for your next day's combo.

Roast chicken plate

Chicken. Cook it. Cool it. Carve it. Team with sharp and soft tastes. Watercress works as it's really peppery. Got anything else that'd go? Customize the combo.

Method

1. Carve a few slices of chicken or get a leg.
2. Mix your mayo with garlic, lemon juice, harissa.
3. Slap on plate with grapes and watercress or whatever.

Combo
Cold roast chicken
Own garlic mayo (page 123) or good bought with crushed clove garlic stirred in
Harissa paste
Lemon juice
Watercress
Grapes

Honey & marmalade gammon plate

Gammon's ideal. It's sweet, fast to carve, lasts, goes with loads. Make it. My brother Tom nicks it to take back to uni. PS It's easy and cheap to grow your own rocket.

Method

1. Carve gammon with sharp knife.
2. Slice tomatoes across.
3. Peel and slice orange.
4. Plate the lot with coleslaw and rocket.

Combo
Slices of good quality home-cooked or ready-cooked ham or gammon
Ripe tomatoes
1 Orange
Coleslaw
Rocket

Roast beef plate

Oh yes, the rock'n'roll of plates. Get the music on. Get your beef medium rare so you get a tender carve and quality combo.

Method

1. Slice beef thin with a sharp carving knife.
2. Plate combo. Eat with great bread'n'butter.

Combo
Cold roast beef
Mustard or horseradish
Rocket
Dill pickle
Balsamic dressing (page 122)

Fast fish

Vacuum-packed fish suits combos. Smoked mackerel. Smoked salmon's cool, but shop around for the one you like. Prawns need eating fast if you buy fresh. Time trick: buy frozen. Defrost when you want 'em.

Combo
Slices good quality
  smoked salmon
Black pepper
1 lemon or lime
Brown or treacle bread
  (page 125)
Butter
Bit of rocket
1 tomato
1 shallot (optional)
Mustard
  dressing (page 122)

Smoked salmon plate

Salmon boosts brain power. Didn't know that? Eat more smoked salmon. Great to eat if you're trawling through revision.

Method
1. Lay salmon on plate. Grind black pepper over it. Add a good squeeze of lime or lemon.
2. Spread bit of butter on your bread.
3. Slice tomato and optional shallot. Slap on plate with rocket.
4. Drizzle dill and mustard dressing on plate or a bit of balsamic vinegar.

Prawn plate

Prawns make for swift eating. Especially fit for girls (says Alice, my non-veggie sister). Sort the speedy marie rose dressing.

Combo
Handful prawns
Dollop of mayo
1 clove garlic, crushed
Tomato ketchup
Squeeze of lemon juice
Black pepper
Iceberg or other lettuce
Lemon wedges to serve

Method
1. Throw prawns in bowl.
2. Mix mayo, garlic, squeeze of lemon, little ketchup.
3. Coat prawns in mayo. Sit them on lettuce. Season with pepper.

Nifty fruit & veg

Rack up a load of great fruit and veg as you work through the book. Like griddled smoky Med veg or fresh fruit salads. Hey – make twice as much and stash it in the fridge for five-minute panics. Other times, slice it fresh as is for speedy eating.

Avocado & pear combo

Don't get your avocado from shampoo and skin stuff. Eat it and maybe you'll glow all over. Drizzle this combo with balsamic dressing (page 122) or go for my cool fast sour cream dressing.

Method

1. Slice up your avocado and pear.
2. Slap sour cream in bowl. Stir in a little bit of white wine vinegar and tarragon to taste. Drizzle over pears.
3. Scatter onion over tomato. Eat with good quality bread.

Combo
1 avocado
1 pear
Sour cream
White wine vinegar
Fresh tarragon, chopped
Tomato, sliced
Red onion, sliced

Hummus & veg plate

Beats crisps. Buy in some tasty hummus or better, make it when you've time (page 37). Team with deli veg (like artichoke hearts, sun-dried tomatoes, olives) and bread or pitta. Or make crudités (sliced raw veg). Veggie sisters Polly and KR's favourite.

Combo
Hummus
Carrots
Celery
Cucumber
Courgettes
Red peppers
Yellow peppers

Method

1. Slap hummus into a bowl. Sit bowl on larger plate.
2. Peel and slice carrots and celery lengthways. Wash and slice courgettes and cucumber lengthways. Halve your peppers. Cut out seeds and joinery. Slice. Arrange veg round hummus.

Combo
Crackers, or bread if you prefer
Assorted nuts
Raisins or sultanas
Pumpkin seeds
Fresh dates
Soft cheese
Apple
Grapes
Celery (optional)
Chutney (optional)
Bit favourite chocolate

Fruit, cheese, nut & chocolate combo
I love this. You can take it anywhere it's so well behaved. It sits at your workstation, or on the sofa. It's got a load of different tastes and textures. It packs in the energy for your sport. Eat with crackers or try it with my champion fast scone bread (page 125). Customize, but prioritize the chocolate.

Method
1. You know how it works. Slap it all on the plate.
2. Enjoy it.

Fruit yogurt combos

In the mood for something sweet and fruity? I eat one of these most days. Keeps me fit and awake – just about. Fruit's cool. Use yogurt as base camp.

Chocolate & banana

You don't need to be a top chef to work this one out, but don't diss it. It's got loads going for it. Brilliant for energy. Top for chocolate.

Method
1. Chuck yogurt into bowl.
2. Cover with sliced bananas.
3. Grate chocolate over it.

Combo
150 ml/5 fl oz pot natural yogurt
1 or 2 ripe bananas
Bit of good quality chocolate

Honey orange biscuit crunch

Made any of my biscuits (page 89) or brandy snaps (page 119)? Crunch those in or use digestive, ginger or amaretti.

Method
1. Chuck yogurt into bowl.
2. Crunch up biscuits. Stir in.
3. Mix in orange (plus all juice) and raisins.
4. Drizzle the lot with honey.

Combo
150 ml/5 fl oz pot natural yogurt
1 orange, peeled and chopped
1 or 2 biscuits
Few raisins
Runny honey

TIME TRICK
Runny honey is faster from a squeezy bottle.

Berry yogurt crunch

Mmm … cool berries make a perfect summer bowl. (Try blackberries, strawberries, raspberries, blueberries.) Loads of power in there to speed your athletics.

Method
1. Chuck washed berries into bowl.
2. Mix yogurt, honey, cereal in another.
3. Tip over berries. Top with more cereal.

Combo
Handful berries of choice
150 ml/5 fl oz pot natural, vanilla or honey yogurt
2 tbsps crunchy cereal
Runny honey

Smoothies & shakes

Smoothies look and taste great. Take seconds to make. Get your fruit down in one. Building yourself up? Use full milk. Keeping fit? Go for semi-skimmed. Don't do dairy? Use soy milk. Make it easy on yourself. Get a hand blender.

My smoothie basic

Method

1. Get soft fruit combo. Wash it. (Use frozen fruit if you can't get fresh.)
2. Peel a banana. Break into bits with fingers. Chuck into tall plastic jug.
3. Drop in fruit combo.
4. Drizzle a bit of honey in there.
5. Stick milk in to cover fruit. Sub in a bit of plain yogurt if you like.
6. Blitz and froth. Drink it.

My breakfast boost

BANANA, RASPBERRY & BLUEBERRY

I get one of these down me most days. Makes a great emergency breakfast with a flapjack. Chuck bits of banana, load of blueberries and raspberries into jug. Tip in half a pint of milk, drizzle honey. Blitz it.

Blackberry

BANANA, BLACKBERRY & RASPBERRY

Brilliant taste – brilliant colour. Sister's favourite. Chuck bits of banana, 3–4 blackberries, handful of raspberries

(or strawberries) into jug. Add half a pint of milk, drizzle honey. Blitz it.

Exotic banana

BANANA, MANGO & RASPBERRY

Special. My mate Tom's dad sells dried mangoes fairtrade-style. His top smoothie. Chuck bits of banana, chopped peeled fresh mango, load of raspberries into jug. Tip in half a pint of milk, drizzle honey. Blitz it.

Strawberry lite

BANANA & STRAWBERRY

Cool, light and frothy. The smoothest smoothie? Chuck bits of banana, good load of strawberries (chopped if huge) into jug. Tip in half a pint of milk, drizzle honey. Blitz it.

Orange boost
BANANA & ORANGE

Subtle – nice light taste. Usually got this stuff hanging about in the fruit bowl. Chuck bits of banana, juice of freshly squeezed orange into a jug. Tip in half a pint of milk – sub in a bit of vanilla yogurt if you like. Drizzle honey. Blitz it.

Tropic
BANANA, PINEAPPLE & ORANGE

Bit like tutti-frutti ice-cream. Use fresh pineapple if you can, but if you'd rather take it in to model it for art... Chuck bits of 1 banana, chunks or chopped rings from small tin pinapple, bit of fresh orange into jug. Tip in half a pint of milk – sub a bit of yogurt if you like. Drizzle honey. Blitz it

Shakes
Make 'em. Get in ice-cream, milk, chocolate, bananas.

Chocolate shake classic
Tastes great. Works as well as a sports drink.

Tip half a pint of milk into jug.
Add 1 tablespoon drinking chocolate and 2 scoops of best chocolate ice-cream.
Blitz in blender or use a hand blender.
Add an extra scoop of ice-cream.

Speedy banana option

Hey, you've always got time. Blitz this one! Replace drinking chocolate with 1–2 bananas. Blitz. Pour. Add an extra scoop of ice-cream.

Toast to go

It's your best mate. Eats well any time. Run it to the bus or eat in and enjoy it. Note: make your own bread for toasting?

For 1
2 slices home-made white, good quality bought, multi-grain, or treacle bread (page 125)
Butter or soy spread (non-dairy) for spreading
Toppings
Sweet: jam, marmalade, marmite, honey
Savoury: hummus (page 37), tapenade (page 123), baked beans

For 1
2 slices good quality white or brown bread
Extra virgin olive oil
1 clove garlic, cut in half
1 ripe tomato, cut in half

> **VARIATION**
> BRUSCHETTA
> At STEP 4 chop 2 ripe tomatoes. Pile on toast with bit of salt, torn basil, drizzle olive oil.

For 1
2 slices good quality white, brown or treacle bread
Little butter
Own (page 117) or good bought lemon curd

For 1
2 slices treacle bread (page 125)
Butter
Marmite or Vegemite

All-time favourite toast basic
Method
1. Set grill to medium, if using.
2. Slice bread thin if using uncut loaf.
3. Slap under grill. Turn when browned and toast other side. Or stick bread into toaster.
4. Soaky toast lovers – spread butter now.
5. Crisp toast lovers – sit toast in rack or prop up to cool before buttering and topping.
6. Toast dippers – cut into fingers.

My tomato & garlic toast
Very Mediterranean breakfast – but that's incidental. Fact is, it's quality. Enjoy any time.
Method
1. Make toast as basic. Slap on plate.
2. Drizzle each toast with little olive oil.
3. Rub garlic over toast.
4. Rub and squeeze half tomato over each piece.
5. Chuck away used tomato. Enjoy.

Jess's lemon curd
Spread Jess's home-style lemon curd on toast. Or on my speedy scone bread (page 125). Try it.
Method
Couldn't be simpler. Toast bread then spread it.

Joe's Marmite & treacle bread
I'm with Joe on this. Sweet bread and salty spread work together.
Method
Make toast. Spread with butter and Marmite.

Dom's peanut butter & banana toast

Dom and I go gymin' it. This power-packer toast builds muscle. Partner with choc shake (page 19).

Method
1. Toast bread. Spread thickly with peanut butter.
2. Top with banana.

For 1
2 slices good quality white, brown or treacle bread (page 125)
1–2 tbsps peanut butter
1 large banana, sliced or mashed

WHY NOT?
Make this as a sarnie, grill as a toastie.

Charlotte's toasted cheese

Speedy, cheesy.

Method
1. Preheat grill to max. Prep cheese.
2. Toast one side of bread. Spread untoasted side with chutney.
3. Top with cheese. Toast till good'n'bubbling.

For 1
2 slices good quality white, brown or treacle bread (page 125)
Mature Cheddar cheese, thinly sliced
Mango chutney (optional)

Hatty's cinnamon toast

Styley! Do the cinnamon mix and fridge for more later.

Method
1. Pre heat grill.
2. Tip butter, sugar and spice together in bowl. Mix to smooth cream using a wooden spoon. Taste, add a bit more cinnamon if you like.
3. Toast one side of bread. Spread untoasted side with mix.
4. Toast spread-side up till hot and bubbling.

For 1
50 g/2 oz soft butter
35 g/1 ½ oz caster sugar
1 tsp cinnamon
1–2 slices white, brown or multi-grain bread

10 minutes Champion

Get your apron on (not compulsory – maybe do what I do: stick a tea towel in your back jeans pocket. Use it when you need to). It's time to get cooking. OK, sarnies don't fall into obvious cordon bleu categories, but they're Michelin star in my house. Every meal's got to be a real event, even if it's slapped together in very little time.

There's some cool stuff here. Feasts on toast to sort you out, dips and pâtés for when you're in that sort of mood. Shed-loads of omelettes. (So they're simple, but the sign of a real chef if you get them right.) Sexy hot and cold salads. Enjoy yourself with the awesome fruit puddings.

Great sarnies

Sarnies? Don't take them for granted. They're marvellous. First off: slap any of my great combo ingredients between bread. That'll work. Second: whack these specials together.

For 1
2 hard-boiled eggs
1 tbsp good or own
  mayo (page 123)
Black pepper
Home-cooked gammon
  (page 120) or good
  quality thin deli ham
Little chilli jam or sweet
  chilli sauce
2 slices treacle (page
  125) or good brown or
  white bread

VARIATION
VEGGIE
Skip the ham.
Substitute chopped
watercress or
tomato.

TIME TRICK

Hard-boil eggs in
advance. To make:
lower eggs into small
pan of boiling water.
Bring back to boil for
10 minutes. Cool
under running water.
Tap to crack and peel
them.

Ham, egg mayo & chilli jam

This one's great when you come back from the gym. Eggs are a cool source of protein. Good for weight training. Builds up muscle.

Method
1. Crack and peel eggs. Mash in small bowl with mayo and pepper.
2. Slice bread (thin for thin ham – thicker for gammon). Spread one slice (or two) with chilli jam/sauce to taste. Spread with egg mayo. Cover with ham or gammon.
3. Sandwich with remaining bread. Delicious.

Fab tuna, spring onion & cucumber wrap

How much flavour can you take? Wrap up a dull day or a yawning morning at school. Tuna mayo gets a cool sushi twist. The ginger and punchy wasabi does it.

For 1
1 x 200 g/7 oz can tuna
2 tbsps mayonnaise (page 123)
1 tbsp wasabi or horseradish sauce
2 spring onions – one chopped, one sliced
10 cm/4 in piece peeled cucumber – half chopped, half sliced
Few sprigs of coriander
4 gratings of fresh peeled ginger or pieces of sushi ginger
Squeeze of lime or lemon
Salt and black pepper
Lettuce or other green leaf
1 wrap

Method

1. Drain tuna. Tip in bowl. Mash with fork. Add mayo and a little wasabi or horseradish. Taste. Add more for punchy flavour.

2. Mix in spring onion, cucumber, coriander, ginger, little lemon or lime juice. Don't make it too wet. Add a little salt and black pepper.

3. Lay wrap flat. Stick lettuce or leaves in centre. Spread tuna mix across.

4. Roll up wrap. Fold each end over and under to seal. Cut in diagonal line across just before eating.

Greek salad pitta

Double physics to face? I'll take sun, sea and this brilliant pitta. Strange how some tastes help you escape. Here you've got feta, herbs, olives, cool salad hanging about in one sparky dressing. Note: olives have loads of iron so could help sort physics.

For 1
75 g/3 oz feta cheese, cubed
1 tbsp extra virgin olive oil
Squeeze of lemon juice
Few sprigs of torn coriander or thyme
Few pitted olives
1 tomato, roughly chopped
5 cm/2 in cucumber, peeled and chopped
10 g/½ oz red onion, chopped small
1 pitta bread

Method

1. Tip feta into bowl. Pour over oil, lemon juice, torn or sprinkled herbs. Turn and leave for few minutes if there's time. Cut stones from olives if not pitted.

2. Ready to eat? Add olives, cucumber, onion and tomato to bowl. Turn once.

3. Warm pitta in toaster till soft and puffy, not stiff. Cut along one side with sharp knife.

4. Spoon cool mix into pitta.

WHY NOT?
Substitute feta with tuna. Stick a hard-boiled egg on top.

TIME TRICK

When roasting chicken (page 121) roast a load more spuds than you need. Stick cold chicken-flavoured roasties in fridge for cooking in omelettes, fry-ups or this pitta.

VARIATION
MUSHROOM PITTA
At STEP 1 fry or griddle four large washed and quartered button mushrooms to substitute potato.

For 1
Sunflower oil for griddling
2 cold cooked potatoes, cubed
1 tsp tandoori powder or turmeric/cumin mix
Squeeze lemon juice
Few sprigs fresh coriander or parsley
1 pitta bread
Mango chutney
Little red onion, chopped small
2 tbsps own (page 37) or bought hummus
Celery, thinly sliced
25 g/1 oz Cheddar, grated
10 g/½ oz raisins

Sizzling spuds and stuff in pitta

May sound weird but tastes pretty brilliant. Cold spuds get an extreme make-over. Fry for soft eating. Griddle for crisp. Stuff your pitta with loadsa great extras. Don't try to be neat, just pile them in. It's like filling your bag before school in the morning.

Method

1. Heat griddle to hot. Brush with little oil. Sprinkle potato cubes lightly in tandoori powder or spices. **Either:** sizzle on griddle for 1–2 minutes each side. Turn with tongs till crisp and cooked through. **Or:** fry spuds in little olive oil and spices. Keep turning till done.
2. Squeeze over a little lemon and torn coriander. Set aside to cool a bit.
3. Heat pitta bread in toaster till soft and puffy, not stiff. Remove. Cut along one side with sharp knife till pocket opens. Spread side with bit of chutney.
4. Slap in hummus, Cheddar, celery, raisins, red onion, potatoes. Eat warm or cold. Delicious.

Club specials

One of the hotel greats – the club sandwich. Treat yourself and your mates, or parents in late. Rules? Get the toast really crisp. Mix'n'match contrasting textures and combo of flavours.

Club one – chicken, ham, tomato, green leaf & mayo

A bit like jenga – how high can you go? Bigger's better, but can you handle it? Note: the tryptophan (Google it) in chicken and ham helps stop you stressing. Or maybe it's just down to piling and stacking.

Method

1. Toast bread. Remove crusts with sharp knife.

2. Spread mayo on one slice, mango chutney on another, optional pesto on another.

3. Stack chicken on mayo toast. Add leaves. Top with second slice of toast.

4. Stack ham and tomato on that slice. Top with final piece of toast.

For 1

3 slices great white bread
Mayo – plain, garlic or harissa (page 123)
Mango chutney
Pesto (optional; page 124)
Chicken slices, from own roast (page 121) or bought
Ham slices, from own gammon (page 120) or bought
Tomato, sliced thinly
Rocket, lettuce or spinach

VARIATION
PANCETTA & AVOCADO CLUB
At STEP 3 replace chicken with avocado. At STEP 4 replace ham with crispy fried pancetta.

For 1

3 slices great white bread
3 slices good quality back,
  streaky or veggie bacon
Little olive oil
1 large egg
1 tomato, thinly sliced
Few sprigs rocket

VARIATION
SALMON CLUB
At STEP 1 spread cream cheese on one slice, lemon mayo on another. At STEP 2 lay smoked or cooked salmon fillet on cream cheese. Add watercress or rocket. At STEP 4 stack more salmon, add a few capers, little chopped shallot, black pepper, drizzle balsamic or fresh lemon.

Club two – egg & bacon

Makes a neat and speedy late-night snack if you're just back from a gig. Can be messy but always tastes lovely.

Method

1. Put grill on high. Toast bread in toaster. Remove crusts with sharp knife.
2. Slap bacon under grill. Reduce heat a bit. Grill till one side done. Turn with tongs. When done (streaky needs a bit longer to crisp) sit it on kitchen paper somewhere warm to wait.
3. Tip olive oil into small frying pan. Heat. Crack egg by tapping it on hard surface. Hold egg between both hands. Stick thumbs into crack. Pull shell apart, holding it just over pan. The egg will slip in neatly. Reduce heat a bit. Use spatula to flick oil over egg yolk. Turn to cook briefly on other side or leave sunnyside up.
4. Stack. Layer egg, bacon, rocket and tomato between three slices of toast. Where's the ketchup?

Sam's special

The ultimate club. All my favourite flavours. Sometimes I'll chuck in an extra ingredient. Always experiment.

For 1
3 slices great white bread
Mayo
Good quality mozzarella cheese (sliced from ball)
2–3 slices Parma ham
Tomato, sliced
Balsamic vinegar
Rocket

Method

1. Toast bread. Remove crusts with a knife. Cool.
2. Spread mayo on two slices.
3. Slice one: mayo side up, lay Parma, mozzarella, tomatoes. Top with slice two with mayo side up.
4. Lay rocket on top. Drizzle with little balsamic.
5. Top with third slice.

Mushroom, rocket & balsamic

A great veggie treat. Field or portobello mushrooms are awesomely cool. Packin' in loads of meaty flavour.

For 1
2 portobello mushrooms
2 cloves garlic, crushed
Salt and black pepper
Little olive oil or soft butter
Lemon juice
Ciabatta or good quality white or brown bread
Rocket or other green leaf
Balsamic vinegar

Method

1. Preheat oven to 230°C/450°F/gas 8.
2. Peel mushrooms or wipe with kitchen paper. Remove stalks. Prick all over with fork.
3. Mix garlic, salt, pepper. Add enough oil or soft butter to spread over the tops of both mushrooms. Put a good squeeze of lemon juice over each one. Slap on baking tray into oven for 10 minutes.
4. After 5 minutes: **Either:** Put griddle on hob. Split ciabatta. Rub little oil on cut surfaces. Griddle these sides till toasted. **Or:** Make toast in toaster.
5. Slap rocket on ciabatta. Top with mushrooms. Drizzle with little balsamic. Top or leave it open.

For 1

1 x 150 g/5 oz fillet or sirloin steak (thin cut – ask a butcher)
1 clove garlic, cut in half
Little olive oil
2 slices great white bread
Sea salt and black pepper

WHY NOT?

Use resting time to make shake, smoothie or juice up some OJ.

TIME TRICK

If you've got time, get meat to room temperature before cooking.

For 1

1 slice bread
Little olive oil
1 egg
2 thin slices mozzarella
2 or 3 fresh basil leaves

Speedy steak

Top sarnie. Team player. Goes with ketchup, mustard. Every time a winner.

Method

1. Get meat from fridge 5 minutes before cooking. Rub with garlic. Brush with little olive oil. Preheat griddle.

2. Slap meat to sizzle on griddle for 1 minute. Turn with spatula. Cook other side for 1 minute for medium rare (tender) or 2 for well done (bit of chew). Remove from pan.

3. Season with little sea salt, pepper. Leave to rest somewhere warm for 2–3 minutes. Slap into bread. Eat alone or with favourite extras.

Cheeky egg & mozzarella open sarnie

Posher-than-your-average fried egg sarnie makes for a wicked eat in revision break. A tasty brain-boosting option. Note: a knife and fork highly recommended.

Method

1. Toast bread.

2. Put oil in small frying pan. Heat. Crack egg on side of pan.

3. Break open with thumbs. Let egg slip into pan. Careful. It splutters.

4. As white begins to set, put one mozzarella slice onto egg white using spatula.

5. Repeat with remaining slice. The cheese will start to melt onto egg. Drop basil leaves on yolk and cheese. Soon as it's done shift onto toast. Tasty.

Luxury fish kebab sandwich

Posh fish on sticks. Very impressive if your granny or girlfriend drop round. Stick fish in between bread with slatherings of mayo, salsa or ketchup. Or eat au naturel with bread'n'butter. Note: really speedy brain food.

Method

1. Preheat grill to high.
2. Tip tuna into one bowl, white fish into another.
3. Mix oil, garlic, herbs, good squeeze of lemon or lime juice, salt and black pepper. Share between fish. Turn well.
4. Leave to rest for 5 minutes. Mix mayos or salsas while you wait.

5. Thread white fish and tuna onto separate metal skewers. Stick under grill. Watch and turn as they cook through 3–4 mins per side; depends on temp and size of chunks.
6. De-skewer to make sarnie. Or serve as is with bread on side. Eat with mayo, ketchup, dips.

For 2

225 g/8 oz firm white fish (haddock or cod), cubed
225 g/8 oz tuna steak, cubed
Olive oil
Lemon or lime juice
1 clove garlic, crushed
Few sprigs parsley or coriander
Salt and black pepper
4 slices of bread
Mayo or mango salsa
Sliced lemon or lime and bay leaves for threading (optional)

WHY NOT?

Make banana and bacon kebab sandwich. Cut 1–2 bananas into 5 cm chunks. Cut 3 rashers of bacon in two. Wrap a piece of bacon around each banana chunk. Thread wrapped pieces on metal skewers. Grill 4 minutes per side. Eat as is or between bread. You can sub fresh dates for bananas.

Home alone on toast

Sometimes just toast just isn't enough. So sort something brilliant to go on it. Make it simple and cheesy. Or get a bit flash with a French or Italian toastie. There's something pizza-y and something spicy here. Toast is cool. Toast is global.

Rabbit on toast

For 2
25 g/1 oz soft butter
110 g/4 oz strong
 Cheddar, grated
1 tsp made mustard
Shake of Worcestershire
 sauce
1–2 tbsps milk or beer
Bit of finely chopped
 spring onion (optional)
2 slices bread

A brilliant snack. Make loads of topping. Cook some now. Store the rest to cook later. (Also great to flavour plain mashed spuds. Or slap it on a field mushroom and bake it.)

Method
1. Preheat grill to medium.
2. Slap all topping ingredients together in a bowl. Cream with a wooden spoon.
3. Grill bread on one side. Spread topping on uncooked side. Cook till bubbling. Great with leaves and chutney.

Baked toasted cheese on garlic ciabatta

For 1
Piece of ciabatta loaf,
 sliced across in two
Butter
1 clove garlic, cut
Few drops white wine or
 tomato for squishing
At least 50 g/2 oz
 Gruyère or Cheddar
 cheese, thinly sliced

Bake toast instead of grilling it. That way you get it crisp on the outside, light in the middle. PS Make industrial amounts of these for video nights, post-footie gatherings, any old party. They're really different and totally delicious.

Method
1. Preheat oven to 230°C/450°F/gas 8.
2. Rub both pieces of bread with garlic. Spread with a little butter.
3. Put on baking tray in hot oven for 5 minutes. Remove.
4. Dribble few drops of wine over each slice or squeeze half a tomato over it. Cover with Gruyère. Bake for another 5 minutes. Magnificent.

VARIATION
FRUITY CHEESE
TOAST
At STEP 4 slap a bit
of chutney on bread
before Gruyère.

Pizza cheese on baked baguette

No home-made pizza about? Don't panic. Make this right now. It tastes great. Mates round? Slap shed-loads of these in the oven for cool speedy pizza addict-style eating.

Method

1. Preheat oven to 230°C/450°F/gas 8.
2. Rub garlic clove on baguette. Drizzle with little olive oil.
3. Put on baking tray in hot oven for 5 minutes.
4. Spread passata or tomato sauce thinly over hot bread.
5. Top with Cheddar or Gruyère. Bake for further 5 minutes. Sprinkle with dried oregano.

For 1
Piece of baguette
  sliced across
Clove garlic, cut
Little olive oil
2 tbsps passata
  with herbs or own
  tomato sauce (page 68)
75 g/3 oz Gruyère or
  Cheddar, sliced across
  or grated
Pinch dried oregano

Eat with: Green salad

VARIATION
ANCHOVY TOASTS
At STEP 4 lay drained anchovy fillets on passata. Top with cheese.

For 1
2 eggs
2 tbsps sour cream
1 tbsp sugar
Good pinch cinnamon
2 slices white bread
Little butter
1–2 rashers streaky
  bacon
1 banana
Few blueberries
Maple syrup

WHY NOT?
Sizzle a slice or two
of peeled butternut
squash on a lightly
oiled hot griddle.
Turn when criss-
crossed. Eat with
crispy bacon and
maple syrup.
Awesome combo.

Hot fruit on French toast (and bacon)

It's your birthday everyday with this cool breakfast. It's got a bit of everything. Spicy sugared toast, soft melty fruit, good old maple syrup and crispy bacon. Note: had a sleepover? Drag them up for this one.

Method

1. Preheat grill. Crack eggs into large shallow bowl.

2. Add sugar, cinnamon, sour cream. Beat well with fork.

3. Dip first slice of bread into mix. Soak both sides then hold over bowl to shake off excess. Repeat with next slice.

4. Melt butter in large frying pan. (Don't burn it.) When bubbling, put eggy breads in to fry till crisp and golden. Turn.

5. Meantime stick bacon under grill. Cook each side till crisp.

6. Slap French toast on plate with bacon. Keep warm.

7. Fry fruit in pan for 1–2 minutes till just soft and oozing. Pile on toast. Drizzle with maple syrup.

Tuna melt

Break out the tuna. Fork it. The tangy bits spritz the tuna fish up. Fast to make; strangely relaxing.

Method

1. Preheat oven to 230°C/450°F/gas 8 or preheat grill.
2. Drain tuna. Mix in bowl with lemon or lime juice, herb, pepper, onion.
3. Rub ciabatta with garlic clove. Drizzle with little olive oil. Sit bread on baking tray in oven for 5 minutes or grill it for 2.

For 1
Piece of baguette or ciabatta, sliced in two across
Little olive oil
Clove of garlic, cut
1 x 200 g/7 oz can tuna
Squeeze lemon or lime juice
Black pepper
Little red onion, chopped small
Fresh coriander, torn
50 g/2 oz Gruyère or Cheddar

4. Spread tuna mix on bread. Top with thin strips of Cheddar or Gruyère. Bake for 5 minutes or grill for 2–3. (Toasting under grill is OK but chewier.)

Mozzarella in Carrozza

Italian "cheese in a carriage". Get a slice of this hot cheese sandwich before you run for the bus. Want to up your speed? Then go with the chilli.

Method

1. Spread one slice of bread with pesto. Another with a bit of chilli jam.
2. Place drained mozzarella slices across the top of the pesto. Top with other slice of bread – chilli side down. Press slices firmly together.
3. Crack egg into wide shallow bowl. Whisk with fork. Add milk and very little salt and black pepper.
4. Heat oil with little butter in frying pan. Dunk sandwich into egg mix to coat both sides well. Hold over bowl so excess drops in. Fry sandwich in pan for 3–4 minutes each side till golden brown. Not a chilli fan? Sub sun-dried tomato paste.

Scrambled egg on toast with asparagus and balsamic

For 1
2 large eggs
1 slice bread
Olive oil for griddling
4 spears asparagus
Knob of butter
Salt and black pepper
Fresh tarragon, parsley
  or basil (optional)
Balsamic vinegar

Plain scramble gets dynamic action. This one's got style. Bend asparagus spears to find out where to snap them…

Method
1. Crack eggs into a bowl. Whisk with a fork. Season.
2. Put griddle on heat. Brush with little olive oil. Griddle asparagus gently, turning, for 5 minutes (or boil for 3–4 mins).
3. Toast bread.
4. Put knob of butter into small pan over gentle heat. Tip in egg mix. Stir like mad with wooden spoon. Remove from heat while eggs are still soft. Season with salt, pepper and optional herbs.
5. Tip onto toast. Lay asparagus on top. Dribble tiny bit of balsamic.

Spicy chickpeas on naan toast with raita

For 1
Little groundnut or
  sunflower oil
1 small onion, chopped
  small
1 clove garlic, crushed
Pinch turmeric
Pinch chilli powder
Pinch cumin
Little salt
Half 400 g/14 oz can
  chickpeas, drained
Few sprigs fresh coriander

Raita
5 cm/2 in piece of
  cucumber, peeled and
  chopped small
3 tbsps yogurt
1 clove garlic, crushed

1–2 mini naan breads,
  plain or garlic and
  coriander
Lemon or lime wedges
Mango chutney

Get a takeaway without sending out for one… Crispy naan bread makes a great plate for soft chickpeas and cool raita.

Method
1. Put frying pan on heat. Tip in a very little oil. Add onion, garlic, turmeric, chilli, cumin, salt. Cook very gently for 2 or 3 minutes. Add chickpeas. Turn to coat. Cook very gently for 5 minutes.
2. Meantime tip yogurt into bowl. Crush in garlic. Add cucumber. Mix.

3. Heat griddle. Smear with very little oil. Split naan in two through the middle. Griddle on one side till crisp as you like. Turn. Griddle other side.
4. Mix fresh coriander into hot chickpeas. Tip mix onto naan. Spoon raita onto side. Squeeze lemon or lime at table with mango chutney.

Pâtés

I've seen girls pick on these. Dip veg sticks in them. Spread them on pittas and crackers. Lads rip open the tortilla chips. Popular choice all round then.

Spicy hummus

Light. Spicy. Nice. Mates want it; sisters too. Who gets it? Maybe not sisters… OK make twice as much… This is your classic hummus but flavourwise it's got a load extra. Note for veggie mates: this powers on protein.

Method

1. Drop garlic, onion, chickpeas and water into food processor. Blitz.

2. Add tahini, honey, lemon juice, spices, coriander, olive oil, little salt.

3. Blitz till smooth as you like it. Add more water, lemon juice, oil to taste. Scrape out into bowl.

4. Drizzle thin layer of olive oil over to seal. Sprinkle with a little paprika for colour. Chill if you can. Keeps in fridge for a week. Great with tortilla chips, toast or pittas warmed in toaster and veg sticks.

For 2–4
3 cloves garlic
25 g/1 oz red onion
400 g/14 oz tin chickpeas, drained
2 tbsps water
1 tbsp tahini
1 tsp honey
Juice of 1–2 lemons
1 tsp sweet paprika
1 tsp ground coriander
Pinch chilli powder
1 tbsp fresh coriander
1 tbsp extra virgin olive oil
Pinch salt
Extra water or olive oil to sort smooth texture

For 2–4
Guacamole
2 large ripe avocados, peeled and stoned
2 green chillis, chopped small
50 g/2 oz red onion, chopped small
2 tomatoes, chopped small
Fresh coriander, torn
Juice of 2 limes or 1 lemon
Salt and black pepper
Pinch cumin (optional)

Garlic pittas
6 small pittas, sliced through
50 g/2 oz soft butter
2 cloves garlic, crushed
Parsley or coriander, finely chopped (optional)

For 2–4
Paté
1–2 smoked trout fillets
1 x 200 g/7 oz pack of cream cheese
1 lemon
Few strands of fresh dill (optional)
Little salt and black pepper

Melba toast
4 slices white bread

VARIATION
TUNA PÂTÉ
At STEP 1 sub a can of tuna (drained) for trout. Blitz as in main recipe. Chop in bits of sushi ginger (optional).

Chunky guacamole & garlic pittas

Get a trolley-load of flavours with this chunky dip. Prefer it smooth? Whizz the lot in a processor with a bit of mayo or cream cheese. Eat it with whatever but why not try it out with these crisp garlic pittas?

Method

1. Preheat oven to 200°C/400°F/gas 6.
2. Dip: Mash avocado roughly in a bowl. Stop while still lumpy. Chuck in chilli, onion, tomato, coriander. Mix lightly. Add lime or lemon juice to taste. Bit of salt, pepper and cumin (if using).
3. Pittas: Mash butter, garlic, herb together. Spread across each pitta half. Stick into oven on baking tray till butter melted and pitta crisping (5–8 minutes).
4. Pile guacamole on warm garlic pittas. PS Pittas not compulsory. Toast or tortilla crisps just as good.

Smoked fish pâté with melba toast

Take the ingredients straight from the fridge. That means you can eat this cool pâté soon as you've blitzed it. (Make the melba toast. It's cool, thin and crunchy.)

Method

1. Paté: Throw smoked trout, half pack of cream cheese, juice of half a lemon, dill, salt into processor. Blitz for few seconds. Taste. Add more cream cheese for smoother taste, more lemon for slightly sharper flavour, and a good twisting of black pepper. Chill in freezer or fridge for 5 minutes. Eat now or chill. Lasts for three days in fridge.

2. Melba toast: Preheat grill. Toast bread in toaster. Remove crusts. Cut sideways through bread with sharp knife till you have separated it into two thin slices. Slide them uncooked side up under medium grill. Watch them curl – not burn. Remove when browned and crisp.

Cold plated salads

Speak for themselves. So I'll shut up then…

Tame tuna & beanie salad

Been sleeping for a few days? No one's had time to get to the shops? Need something sparky to eat? Get cans of beans and tuna out of the cupboard. Wake up with a few crunchy bits and a really cool dressing.

Method

1. Boil small pan of water. Add green beans. Boil for 3–4 minutes till just crisp. Drain under cold water. Chop or leave whole.

2. Chuck garlic, sugar, salt, mustard, vinegar into small bowl. Mix. Add oil, beating or whisking.

3. Chuck green beans, canned beans, onion, celery and cherry tomatoes into large bowl. Chuck dressing over. Mix. Leave till ready to eat.

4. Drain tuna. Fork gently into bean salad. Eat with loadsa warmed bread to soak up the dressing.

For 2

50 g/2oz green beans
1 clove garlic, crushed
Pinch sugar
Pinch salt
½ tsp Dijon mustard
1 tbsp wine vinegar
3 tbsps olive oil
410 g/14 oz can cannellini or haricot beans, drained
1 small red onion, sliced
1 stick celery, sliced
Few cherry tomatoes, halved
Few fresh herbs of choice – coriander, parsley, basil
200 g/7 oz can tuna

WHY NOT?

Slap on a hard-boiled egg and a dollop of mayo.

10 minutes

VARIATIONS
CHICKEN CAESAR
At STEP 5 throw left-
over roast chicken
(page 121) or fresh
griddled chicken bits
(page 76) onto mix.
BACON CAESAR
At STEP 5 fry up 4–6
rashers streaky bacon
till brown and crisp.
Drain on kitchen
paper. Cut or crumble
over lettuce.
SPEEDIER CAESAR
At STEP 4 slap garlic
and lemon juice to
taste in quality
bought mayo.

For 4
2–3 slices white bread,
   baguette or ciabatta
Little olive oil
1 garlic clove, cut
1 large cos lettuce

Dressing
2 eggs
2 cloves garlic
4 anchovy fillets
2 tbsps lemon juice
1 tsp wine vinegar
Good pinch mustard
   powder
1 tsp Worcestershire
   sauce
125 ml/4 oz sunflower
   oil
50 ml/2 oz olive oil
1 tbsp water

Parmesan, cut thin

Caesar salad

One of the world's classics. Crunchy lettuce, garlic croutons, punchy creamy dressing. Celebs eat it. I eat it. Cheats buy the dressing. Chefs make their own. What's the difference? I can't describe it. Toss salad with your hands to coat leaves properly.

Method

1. Croutons: Preheat oven to 220°C/425°F/gas 7. Drizzle little oil on baking tray. Rub with garlic. Chop bread into crouton chunks. Chuck onto tray. Turn to coat in oil. Bake for 8 minutes or till crisp as you like it.

2. Salad: Tear cos. Wash well. Drain. Chuck in large bowl.

3. Egg: Boil small pan water. Lower eggs in. Boil for one minute. Remove.

4. Dressing: Crush garlic and anchovies in small bowl with pestle or wooden spoon. Crack eggs open. Spoon yolks into bowl. (Ditch shell and whites.) Add lemon juice, wine vinegar, mustard powder, Worcestershire sauce. Whisk together with balloon whisk. Sit bowl on tea towel. Measure oils into jug. Pour oil drip by drip into yolk mix, whisking madly as you go so it thickens. When half used, add a bit more at a time till creamy. Add water to stabilize.

5. Assemble: Tip dressing over torn lettuce leaves. Turn with your hands (lovely). Toss. Chuck croutons in. Turn or leave them sitting. Cut loads of Parmesan from a piece. Scatter over salad. Use knife or potato peeler.

Chicken tonnato salad

Enjoy yourself with this really sexy Italian-style salad. Make over some cold roast chicken. Trinny and Susannah it with a good bit of salad and tuna mayo.

Method

1. Chuck dressing ingredients into processor. Blitz till smooth. Taste. Adjust flavour.

2. Slice chicken thinly. Lay on plate. Drizzle with tonnato dressing. Surround with rocket, olives and cherry tomatoes. Drizzle balsamic if you like it.

3. Eat with good crusty bread. Store extra dressing in fridge.

Curried chicken waldorf salad

Awesome. Classic cold roast meets classic waldorf in a curried mayo. Veggies use hardboiled eggs instead. Makes a versatile all-year-round power-packing salad.

Method

1. Mix all dressing ingredients together in a bowl. Taste and adjust so you get it as you like it.

2. Add apple, celery and grape to mix, with any optional raisins or other fruit.

3. Now chop chicken into bite-size bits and add to mix. Or carve and serve dressed fruit on the side with rocket and cherry tomatoes. Great with warm brown or treacle bread and a bit of butter.

For 1–2
Tonnato dressing
4 tbsps home-made or good bought mayo
Half 200 g/7 oz can tuna, drained
2 anchovies, drained
1 clove garlic, crushed
Few capers, drained
1 tbsp lemon juice

Chicken salad
Few slices cold roast chicken or baked or griddled chicken fillet
Rocket leaves
Black olives
Cherry tomatoes
Balsamic vinegar (optional)

For 1–2
Dressing
4 tbsps home-made or good bought mayo
1 clove garlic, peeled and crushed
Good squeeze of lemon
1 tsp mango chutney
½–1 tsp curry paste
½ tsp tomato ketchup

Waldorf salad
1 crisp apple, peeled and chopped
2 sticks celery, chopped small
Few grapes, halved
Few raisins (optional)
Fresh mango or peach (optional)
Cold chicken from a roast or cooked chicken breast or leg
Rocket or other green leaves
Cherry tomatoes

Hot plated salads

These are controversial. (Not.) There's nothing wrong with a hot and cold salad.

For 1

110 g/4 oz halloumi
Bit of olive oil
Good squeeze lime or lemon juice
Black pepper
Few leaves of coriander, mint, oregano, chopped
2 ripe tomatoes, thinly sliced
Small red onion, thinly sliced
Rocket or other salad leaves
Pitted black olives (optional)
Extra virgin olive oil

Eat with:

Pitta bread and salad
Piece of griddled or baked garlic ciabatta
A heap of my tasty couscous salad (page 69).

WHY NOT?

Try hot goats' cheese salad. Toast bits of baguette. Spread with any goats' cheese. Toast under medium grill for 5 minutes or till lightly browned. Slap onto salad. Dress the lot in my sparky dressing (page 122). Toss a few walnuts in there if you like 'em.

Sizzled halloumi & cool green leaves

Is it a cheese or a bar of soap? Griddle it. Then slap it hot on top of this simple cool salad.

Method

1. Cut halloumi into 5 mm/¼ in slices. Lay on plate. Brush or drizzle with little olive oil.

2. Throw salad leaves, tomato, onion, half the herbs, and optional olives into a bowl. Drizzle with little olive oil. Toss.

3. Preheat griddle. Lay slices of halloumi to cook. Turn with palette knife after 1–2 minutes or when char-grilled and golden. Cook other side.

4. Squeeze with lime or lemon juice. Season with black pepper and reserved herbs.

5. Heap salad on plate. Drop cheese on top.

For 1
1–2 slices bread
 (ciabatta good but any
 works)
Olive oil for greasing
1 clove garlic, cut across

Dressing
1 tsp English or French
 mustard
Good pinch sugar or
 drizzle honey
Pinch sea salt
Juice ½ lemon
2–3 tbsps olive oil

Salad
Olive oil for frying
1 slice black pudding
2 slices bacon, streaky
 for crisp; back for soft,
 or pancetta, sliced or in
 chunks
Good handful washed
 green leaves – frissée
 lettuce classic but cos,
 rocket, or spinach work

VARIATION
POACHED
EGG'N'BACON PILE
At STEP 1 bake single
thick slice of bread or
ciabatta. At STEP 5 sit
bread on plate. Pile
salad on top. Fill
small frying pan two-
thirds full with water.
Boil. Turn heat down.
Crack 1 egg into cup.
Swirl simmering
water with wooden
spoon. Tip egg into
swirl. Let it poach for
3 minutes. Lift out of
water on slotted
spoon. Sit on salad
pile. Drizzle with little
more dressing.

All day breakfast salad

Fit eating meets fit fry-up. Who wins? You do. This one's full of cracking tastes. OK, so black pudding's not everyone's cup of tea but I love it. PS Anyone asks, you're having salad.

Method

1. Preheat oven to 220°C/425°F/gas 7. Drizzle bit of oil and rub garlic over baking tray. Cut bread into cubes. Chuck onto tray. Roll to coat. Bake for 8 minutes or till crisp as you like.

2. For dressing: Put mustard in small bowl with honey or sugar, salt. Mix well. Stir in lemon juice. Whisk in oil. Or shake the lot up in a jar.

3. Put little oil in frying pan. Add black pudding. Fry gently each side till hot (bought stuff is already cooked so don't overdo). Or grill/heat through in the oven till done.

4. Put bacon in pan and cook till crisp/soft as you like. Remove. Chop bacon and pudding into bits.

5. Throw lettuce into bowl. Chuck in dressing. Toss to coat well (use your fingers). Add bacon, pudding, croutons. Mix together.

Flash omelettes

These babies travel: to the table, the sofa, even the great outdoors. Make them new-style and light. Use a variety of oils for cooking. Be inventive with fillings. Eat hot or cold. Stick them in bread, on bread. Dip or flip them. Style and plate them.

For 1
1 tbsp sesame oil
2–3 spring onions, sliced
25 g/1 oz beansprouts
1 clove garlic, sliced
2–3 button mushrooms, sliced
1 chilli, de-seeded and sliced (optional)
2–3 gratings fresh ginger (optional)
Fresh coriander, torn
Pinch caster sugar
Squeeze lime or lemon juice
2 large eggs
Salt and black pepper
Ginger teriyaki sauce (page 53) or good quality bought one

Flip top, stir-fry omelette

A cool stir-fry in a thin egg wrap. Yessss! Chinese-style revolutionary omelette. Note: I use a 10-inch shallow frying pan for this one.

Method

1. Heat little sesame oil in non-stick pan. Chuck in onion, beansprouts, garlic, mushrooms, chilli and ginger if using. Stir-fry gently for 2–3 minutes till softening but still a bit crisp. Add little coriander, sugar, lime. Stir. Remove from pan.

2. Add little more oil if needed. Beat seasoned eggs in bowl with rest of coriander and spring onion.

3. Chuck into pan. Bubble. Tilt to set. Draw set egg aside with fork to let rest cook through if you need to. Should take no more than 45 seconds. When still bit soft and runny on top throw stir-fry in. Flip over. Tip onto plate. Drizzle with teriyaki. Serve.

VARIATIONS
Other excellent flip-top fillings:
✱ 3 cheeses – Cheddar, Gruyère and Parmesan
✱ Crumbled goats' cheese, bit of apple chutney and rocket
✱ Mushroom
✱ Crispy fried bacon or pancetta and rocket
✱ Fried banana with honey drizzle

Punchy chorizo omelette

Chorizo sausage and chilli oil pack a real punch which works really well with this laid-back omelette. Eat on crisped bread. If you're in a lighter mood? Skip the bread. Get some fit salad leaves out and plate it.

Method

1. Preheat oven to 200°C/400°F/gas 6 if eating with bread. Heat bread till warmed through.
2. Heat little oil in omelette pan. Fry chorizo 1–2 minutes each side till just cooked. Remove. Beat seasoned eggs in bowl with fork.
3. Increase heat under pan till bubbling. Chuck eggs in. Tilt to set. Draw set egg aside with a fork so the unset bit can cook if you need to.
4. Chuck chorizo onto egg while still a bit soft. Add the rocket and a smidge of chilli oil. Flip omelette in two or roll.
5. Stick onto hot, crisp, sliced focaccia, into baguette, or plate with salad. Drizzle with a little chilli oil and balsamic.

For 1
Baguette or focaccia (optional)
Little olive oil
10 cm/4 in piece chorizo sausage, sliced
2 large eggs
Rocket
Chilli oil
Balsamic vinegar

Omelette stuffed in baguette with green leaves

Slap some mustard in your egg to lift the flavour. That way it'll stand up to all your relishes. Works hot or cold so maybe stick it in your rucksack for scoffing later…

Method

1. Preheat oven to 200°C/400°F/gas 6. Heat baguette till warmed through.
2. Beat seasoned eggs in bowl with fork. Add mustard. Beat lightly.
3. Heat olive oil in non-stick pan. When hot, chuck eggs in. Bubble. Tilt to cover. Draw set egg aside with fork to let rest cook through if you need to. Remove while top's still a bit soft. Slap on plate. Roll or fold it.
4. Cut baguette across. Slather side with ketchup/pesto/mango chutney. Add green leaves and omelette. Drizzle with sparky dressing (page 122).

For 1
1 baguette
Little olive oil
2 large eggs
1–2 tsps Dijon or English mustard
Salt and black pepper
Rocket or green leaves
Organic tomato ketchup
Mango chutney (optional)
Pesto (optional)
Balsamic dressing

VARIATION
At STEP 4 throw in gammon, Parma or wafer-thin ham. Slather baguette with more mustard.

For 1
Little olive oil
2 large eggs
Basil or parsley (optional)
Salt and black pepper
1 tomato, thinly sliced
Rocket
5 olives
Parmesan, thin sliced
  or curled
Balsamic vinegar

WHY NOT?
Try the sandwich.
Make two omelettes.
Lay flat. Slather one
with bit of tomato
sauce or garlic or
harissa mayo. Top
with filling of choice
then other omelette.

TIME TRICK

For the fastest
perfect poached
egg, put small pan
of water to boil. Tear
off a largish piece of
clingfilm and sit it in
a bowl. Grease
clingfilm lightly with
sunflower oil. Crack
egg into bowl.
Gather edges of
clingfilm together
and twist to seal egg
in. Lift into boiling
water for 3 minutes.
Turn onto toast or
eat with cold sliced
gammon (page 120).

Pizza-style omelette

No pizza dough about? Top a warm or cool omelette with rocket, tomato, Parmesan or whichever express pizza combos you want. Note: I use a little 15-cm/6-inch pan for this one.

Method

1. Beat eggs in small bowl. Add torn herbs if using. Season.
2. Heat olive oil in non-stick pan. When hot, chuck eggs in. Bubble. Tilt to cover. Draw set egg aside with a fork to let the rest cook through if you need to. While top's still a bit soft, slide out onto plate or greaseproof paper.
3. Leave to cool a bit. Top with tomato, rocket, Parmesan shavings. Drizzle with little extra virgin olive oil and balsamic (or own-style pizza toppings, ham, etc). Lovely.

Cool omelette dippers

Take your thin omelette. Roll it up tight. Let it cool. Dip into sauces. PS Do production lines of these for gatherings or parties. Cook ahead and fridge 'em.

Method

1. Make omelettes one at a time. Chuck one egg in a bowl. Beat with fork. Add seasoning and herbs (if using).

2. Heat olive oil in pan. Chuck egg in. Bubble. Tilt to cover. Draw set egg aside with fork to let rest cook through if you need to. Remove omelette while top's still soft. Cool on greaseproof paper. Roll and dip.

Makes 8
Little olive oil
8 eggs
Tarragon, parsley, coriander or basil (optional)
Salt and black pepper

Dips
Sweet chilli sauce
My sparky dressing (page 122)
Teriyaki lime sauce

Flat fried omelette with potato & courgette

A thick omelette. Brightens your brain and your day up. Slice cake style. Share with a lad or a lass. Parent in late (they owe you). This one's also great cold in a picnic or pack-up.

Method

1. Heat olive oil. Lightly fry onions and garlic till soft – not coloured.

2. Chuck in potato and courgette. Cook and turn for a few minutes till crisping up.

3. Beat eggs in bowl with fork. Add herbs, salt and pepper. Add eggs to veg. Use fork to manipulate egg mix gently so that the runny stuff can start to set. Leave to cook through gently. If you want the top golden stick under a preheated grill for 1 minute. Drizzle with bit of chilli oil. Great hot, warm or cold.

For 4
2 tbsps olive oil
6 spring onions, sliced
2 cloves garlic, crushed
2 cold cooked potatoes, small cubes
1 courgette, small chunks
6 eggs
Salt and black pepper
Handful fresh tarragon coriander or parsley, chopped, or sprinkling dried oregano
Little chilli oil

VARIATIONS
NO POTATO
At STEP 2 skip spuds, use 3 chunked courgettes. At STEP 3 add grated Parmesan, Cheddar or Gruyère.
ASPARAGUS
At STEP 2 boil 225 g/ 8 oz thin asparagus (ends trimmed) for 3–4 minutes. Drain. Chop each into 3. Add to cooked spuds.

10 minutes

Fit & fruity

**Fruit's so good it's almost embarrassing. But eat it anyway.
Get yourself healthy for the next match, exam or party.**

For 1
Use any soft or very ripe
  fruit you fancy. Like:
Banana, sliced in two
  lengthways
Peach, stoned and sliced
Plum, stoned and sliced
Nectarine, stoned and
  sliced
Strawberries
Blueberries
Raspberries
Drizzle of apple juice,
  white wine or cider

Eat with: a crisp biscuit
(page 89). Good with
best vanilla, coconut or
cinnamon ice-cream.

Fruit in a paper parcel

Eat this – don't post it. Aside from the mess it'd be a waste.
Parcelled fruit softens up and bakes in its own juices. Serve
and eat from unwrapped parcel. Note: impress yourself plus
any girls around.

Method

1. Preheat oven to 220°C/425°F/gas 7.
2. Cut a large square (at least 35 cm/14 in each side) of baking or
greaseproof paper for each parcel. Fold the piece in half to create a
crease down the middle. Open it back up.
3. Prepare fruit. Leave small fruit such as blueberries, strawberries and
raspberries whole.
4. Lay the fruits on one side of the folded line. Drizzle with a few drops of
apple or other juice. Fold the paper over so the fruit is covered. Then turn
each edge up and in so the fruit is loosely contained. Bake for 8–10
minutes or till done. (Larger harder bits may take 2 extra minutes.)

Pick & mix fruit salad

How many fruits make a salad? Who cares? Note: get a whole range of colours in there. Red and orange fruit are particularly dynamic. Vitamin C gets all the iron in your food going. Sharpens your thinking and your immune system.

Method

1. Wash soft fruit. Rip stalks from strawberries, Chinese gooseberries. Peel kiwi, apple, pear, pineapple, orange, satsuma, banana. Peel and stone mango, peach, nectarine. Stone fruit such as cherry and plum. Brush apple, pear, banana with a little lemon juice to stop browning.
2. Chop to required size. Leave grapes whole or cut in half. Chuck in bowl.
3. Like a bit of liquid in there? Squeeze a bit of fresh orange juice or pour some apple juice in there. **Got some time?** Squeeze more lemon juice over. Sprinkle with a little caster sugar. Leave and the fruit starts to ooze its own juices.

Some ideas:
Green and red grapes
Kiwi fruit
Raspberries
Strawberries
Melon
Mango
Pineapple
Orange
Banana
Satsuma
Blueberry
Chinese gooseberry
Blackberry
Pear
Bit of apple

TIME TRICK

Make loads. Save time for fit-next-day breakfast or pack-up.

Hot banana toast pudding

I invented this when there was nothing much in. Try it. It's unexpectedly cool. The banana softens up and gets buttery. The crisp toast soaks up the fruity syrupy juices.

Method

1. Toast bread. Cut crusts off. Prop up so it stays crisp.
2. Slice two-thirds of the banana down the middle lengthways. Chop rest. Melt butter in small pan. Cook banana gently till browned on one side. Turn. Cook other side till cooked through but still holding shape.
3. Slap orange juice into pan. Then lemon juice. Let it bubble but not dry up. Plate toast. Pile banana on top. Pour juice over. Drizzle with maple syrup.

For 1
1 slice good quality white bread, thinly sliced
25 g/1 oz butter
1 large banana
2 tbsps fresh orange juice
2 tbsps fresh lemon juice
Maple syrup

Eat with: good quality vanilla ice-cream, or a dollop of crème fraîche.

15 minutes Celebrate

Everyone gets their 15 minutes of fame, so get yours with some five-star cooking. (That's mains, sauce, veg, salad, dressing.)

So you'll need to get the timing right. Spuds, for example, take longer than your steak. Obvious, I know, but get them on first.

Yes, it's time for the big hitters. Brilliant beef and lamb. Lovely speedy sauces like salsa verde, ginger teriyaki, sweet'n'sour red jelly. Fish done loadsa ways. Magnificent vegetables. Stir-fries. Noodles. Couscous. Tabbouleh. Clock up extra time for the lushest fruit puddings.

Griddled meat

Griddled meat's a lean mean energy machine. Can't beat it...

For 4
4 x 150 g/5 oz fillet,
 sirloin or rump steak
 (1.5 cm thick)
1 garlic clove, halved
Olive oil
Salt and black pepper

Eat with:
Speedy fried spuds
Couscous
Tomato salad
Onion salad
Green leaves
Stir-fry greens
Creamy mash (page 86)
Noodle cake (page 65)

VARIATIONS
THE ITALIAN
Squeeze lemon over
steak at table.
THE FIREWORK
Stick a piece of
thyme on steak.
Light at table.
PUNCHY MAYO
Mix mayo (page 123)
with one of the
following to taste:
crushed garlic,
lemon juice, wasabi
paste, horseradish,
mustard or harissa.
Stick it to the side.
SOUR CREAM &
CHIVE
Snip chives into
sour cream. Slap on
the side.

Brilliant basic steak

Top choice. Steak can be beautiful. It's simple. Quick. Packed with flavour. Treat it with respect, it'll be what you want it to be. Buy it well. Fillet (lean, expensive, ask for thin cut). Sirloin (good and tasty). Rump (full flavour, texture). Cook it right. Basic steak's speedy so prep the rest of your meal before you get griddling.

Method

1. Rub steaks with garlic. Turn in a few drops of olive oil. Season with pepper.
2. Get griddle very hot. Bang steaks down. Sizzle for 1 minute.
3. Turn with tongs. Sizzle for 1 minute. Repeat till cooked to your taste. I like medium rare (still pink inside). Get it right by looking and testing with a knife.
4. Sprinkle with bit of salt. Let steak relax in warm place for 2 minutes to tenderize.

Ginger teriyaki drizzle

Gorgeous. Top sauce for beef. (Chuck it on salmon and tuna and as a marinade for tofu.) My signature dish. Eat with noodle cake (page 65) and stir-fry.

For 2–4 steaks
2 tsps caster sugar
5 tbsps soy sauce
3 tbsps rice vinegar
Small knob fresh root
  ginger
Few coriander leaves,
  chopped (optional)

Method

1. Mix soy, sugar, rice vinegar. Stir well. Add ginger and coriander to mix.
2. Drizzle over sliced steak cooked as basic.

Steak with lemon, parsley & garlic rub

Sexy. Get your fingers good and garlicky. Really rub this in. Also works on your lamb and tuna.

For 2 steaks
1 clove garlic, crushed
Few leaves rosemary,
  chopped
Sea salt and black
  pepper
Juice of ½ lemon
1 tbsp olive oil

Method

1. Chuck garlic, herb, salt, pepper into pestle and mortar (or mix in bowl).
2. Slap in lemon and oil. Mix to paste. Rub all over meat. Leave 10 minutes. Cook as basic.

Chilli spice mustard beefsteak

The hot one! Eat with a bit of sour cream or mix of crème fraîche and wholegrain mustard.

For 2 steaks
1 clove garlic, crushed
2 tsps Worcestershire
  sauce
Juice of ½ lemon
1 tsp dry mustard
1 tsp sweet paprika
Sea salt and black
  pepper
Few crushed dried chillis
1 tbsp olive oil

Method

Mix everything in a bowl. Rub really well into your meat. Leave 10 minutes. Cook as basic.

Peppered steak

A kick-ass dish. Eats well with pak choi, and speedy fried potatoes (page 61). No beef? Whack it on a pork chop.

For 2 steaks
1 tsp whole or cracked
  black peppercorns
1 tbsp olive oil
1 clove garlic, crushed
Little fresh ginger, grated
  (optional)
Sea salt
Sauce
2 tbsps red wine or
  grape juice
1–2 tbsps double cream
  or crème fraîche

Method

1. Crack whole peppercorns with pestle and mortar. Not too fine or they burn.
2. Slap oil on a plate with garlic and ginger. Rub steak in oil. Add peppercorns, pressing into each side. Rest for 10 minutes while you prep veg or salad.
3. Cook steak to taste in frying pan as basic recipe. Season with little salt. Remove meat and rest. Tip wine or juice to bubble in hot pan. Let it reduce and get sticky. Add cream. Stir and boil. Tip over meat.

For 2

2 lamb steaks or
  2 x 2 lean chump or
  loin chops (these are
  larger chops) or 3 x 2
  neat lamb cutlets
1 tbsp olive oil
Fresh mint, thyme, basil,
  sage or rosemary,
  chopped
1–2 cloves garlic, crushed
Sea salt and black
  pepper

Sauce

3 tbsps redcurrant jelly
3 tbsps orange juice
1 tbsp lemon juice
1 tsp wine vinegar
Few gratings fresh
  ginger
Few gratings orange rind

WHY NOT?

Make mint sauce.
Blitz 2 tablespoons
fresh mint, 1 x 150
ml/5 fl oz tub
natural yogurt, 1
clove garlic, salt.
Eat with lamb.

VARIATIONS

LAMB SPRINKLE
At STEP 2, finely chop
2 cloves garlic, 1 tbsp
parsley, 2 tbsps mint,
grated rind 1 lemon.
Mix together with salt
and pepper. Spinkle
over cooked lamb.
PESTO
At STEP 4, smear
good quality bought
or own pesto (page
124) over grilling
lamb 1 minute
before it's done.
Delicious.

Brilliant lamb basic with sweet & sour red jelly

Griddle or grill it. Lamb's a rich meat so it can take the heat and strong flavours. Try it with this quick sweet jelly. Note: lean protein helps you keep in shape and build up your six-pack (weird!). The iron in lamb helps give you focus. Try this sauce with roast duck, gammon, pork chops and sausages.

Method

1. Mix oil, herb, garlic, salt, pepper together. Rub into lamb. Leave it.

2. Slap sauce ingredients into a pan. Stir gently till thickening. Taste. Adjust adding more jelly to sweeten, or vinegar to get the balance.

3. Meantime, preheat grill to max or heat griddle.

4. Grilling? Sit meat 8 cm/3 inches from heat. Cook 3 minutes for thinner cuts. Turn. Baste with juices. Grill 3 minutes. Lamb is best still pink inside. Test with a knife. Thick chops and steaks need longer. **Griddling?** As steak basic, slap meat down. Sizzle each side till cooked as you like.

5. Leave meat to rest. Drizzle hot jelly over chops. Great with spuds, char-grill veg, peas, beans.

Lamb salsa verde

Lush. Looks like mushed up lawn. It loves lamb and beef, chicken, styley on griddled veg, pasta. Dunk your cheese soufflé in it. Drizzle on tuna. Classic and brilliant.

For 4 steaks
3 cloves garlic
1 bunch parsley
1 bunch basil
1 ½ tbsps capers, rinsed
1 tbsp Dijon mustard
1 tbsp white wine
  vinegar
6–8 tbsps extra virgin
  olive oil

Method
1. Before you cook meat, blitz garlic, parsley, basil, capers, mustard and wine vinegar in a processor.
2. Add oil drizzled very slowly through funnel till you get mayo-style mix.
3. Cook any cut of lamb as basic. Drizzle salsa over meat or slap on the side. Store in fridge. Stir before serving. Make it. Amazing.

Middle Eastern style lamb

I go for lamb steaks this way. Slice onto couscous, tabbouleh, tomato and red onion salad. Eating al fresco? Stuff into pitta.

For 4 steaks
200 ml/7 fl oz natural
  yogurt
2 cloves garlic, crushed
1 tsp ground cinnamon
1 tbsp ground cumin
1 tbsp ground coriander
Salt and black pepper
Fresh coriander

Method
1. Slap half yogurt, spices, garlic, seasoning in shallow bowl. Rub into lamb.
2. Leave till ready to cook. Preheat grill or griddle.
3. Cook as basic. It browns up. Don't panic. Meat may take a bit longer as it's coated. Stick knife in to check it's done as you like. Slice if you want. Sprinkle with fresh coriander, rest of yogurt.

Swift griddled fish

Fish really sorts you out. It sharpens your brain and keeps you fit. When it's fresh it tastes of what it is. For griddling or pan-fry get salmon and tuna steaks or those neat salmon fillets.

For 2
2 x 150–175 g/5–6 oz
   tuna steaks or 2
   salmon fillets, skinned
   and bone-free
Little olive oil
Sea salt and black
   pepper
Lime or lemon

Eat with: noodle cake (page 65) and stir-fry (page 63). Or with salsa; baby spuds; watercress; sliced cucumber with sugar, dill and white wine; garlic mayo (page 123).

VARIATIONS
SESAME FISH
Marinate fish in a mix of lime or lemon juice, crushed garlic, little sesame oil. Cook as basic with few drops of soy added to bubble at last minute.
SALSA FOR SALMON
Prep before you cook. Roughly chop some ripe tomatoes. Stir into my sparky dressing (page 122) with chopped black olives and fresh herb. Pile on your salmon and team with lime and sour cream.

Brilliant basic salmon & tuna

Salmon's kind of flaky, cool, pink and a bit sexy (like some girls I know). Tuna's macho, dark red, meaty. Cooking them couldn't be simpler or faster. Prep veg and salad before cooking fish. PS Don't overload with oil. They bring their own to the party.

Method

1. Preheat griddle, frying pan or grill to max. Check salmon for bones. Yank stray ones out with tweezers. Brush fish with a little olive oil. Season.

2. Slap fish on griddle or pan, or under grill. Cook one side. Turn and cook till done as you like it.

3. Tuna: get it seared outside, and pink in the middle. Overcooking makes it leathery. Test with a knife and watch it. Cook 2 minutes each side as rough guide but could be less.

Salmon: get it seared outside, just cooked through, moist and easily flaking. Test it. Fish will cook in residual heat so don't overdo it.

4. Slap on plate.

Tuna with ginger lime fish drizzle

Treat your tuna to a sparky drizzle. Like jazz, it's got a range of whacky tastes. When it hits the fish they all come together. Also works well with beefsteak.

Method

1. Stick everything in a jar. Shake it. Use or store for a week.

2. Cook tuna as basic. When cooked, drizzle sauce over.

For 2 tuna steaks
2 tsps caster sugar
2 tbsps fish sauce
1 tbsp oyster sauce
1 tbsp Chinese rice wine
  or vinegar
Juice of 3 limes
A few rough gratings of
  ginger
Few leaves of coriander,
  chopped

Eat with: stir-fry and noodle cake (page 65).

Cajun spiced salmon

Get a dry take on your salmon with this one. Lovin' it.

Method

1. Bash all ingredients into a paste in pestle and mortar.

2. Coat both sides of fish. Pan-fry or griddle as basic.

3. Serve with chunks of lime and mayo mixed with sour cream and grated lime.

For 4 salmon fillets
1 tbsp paprika
1 tsp chilli powder
½ tsp cumin
½ tsp allspice
2 tbsps dried oregano
1 tbsp dried thyme
Cracked black
  peppercorns or fresh
  black pepper
Pinch of sea salt
Little olive oil
Little runny honey
  (optional)

Cracking griddled fish chunks

These beauties are great for dipping in ginger teriyaki (page 53) and sweet chilli sauce. Chunking gives fish a change of identity.

Method

1. Chop fish into chunks.

2. Mix rest of ingredients. Roll chunks in mix to coat.

3. Slap on a very hot griddle. Turn with tongs till done. Tuna pink inside. Salmon seared, moist, flaky.

4. Dip as above or slap in salad bowls with croutons, cherry tomatoes, spring onion, cucumber, sparky dressing (page 122).

For 2
2 tuna steaks or
  salmon fillets
Olive oil
Juice of 1 lemon
Salt and pepper
Finely chopped dill,
  parsley, coriander

 **TIME TRICK**

Always do a bit more salmon than you need. Make yourself a next-day salad box, wrap or styley sandwich.

Otherway fish

Want a fast white fish? Get to a good fishmonger and treat yourself to a fillet. Grill it. Buying a whole fish? Check for fresh smell. Bright eyes. Pink gills. We're talking fish by the way – not you in the mirror.

For 2
2 small trout
2 garlic cloves, thinly sliced
1 unwaxed lemon
2 sprigs of rosemary or 4 of dill
White wine, white grape or apple juice
Sea salt and black pepper
Little olive oil
Black olives and extra sliced garlic (optional)

Eat with: speedy fried spuds and green beans

VARIATION
CHINESE-STYLE TROUT
At STEP 3 season inner fish with soy. Stuff with a bit of sliced spring onion, garlic, beansprouts, coriander. Slip a bit of sliced garlic and ginger into wine or juice. Bake as basic.

Speedy baked trout

Pick out a good looking trout for tea on the way home. The fishmonger'll scale and gut it. If you want he'll take out the backbone but I'd keep it in. Bones make for tastier fish. Just don't swallow them.

Method

1. Preheat oven to 200°C/400°F/gas 6.

2. Wash trout under cold running water. Get the inside clean and free of any bits. Drain in colander.

3. Brush a shallow ovenproof dish with oil. Sit fish in side by side. Season insides with pepper, salt, little lemon juice then stuff with garlic, 2 thin slices lemon, whole herbs.

4. Pour wine or juice into dish till halfway up the fish. Add optional olives and garlic. Cover with foil. Slap in the oven for 10 minutes. Remove foil. Cook another 5 minutes. Remove.

5. Test with point of a knife. Fish should be moist and cooked through.

6. Plate fish. Eat with care.

Yorkshire fried fish

A legendary fried fish supper. Batter doesn't matter. Garlic crumb seals in flakes of gorgeous white fish. Team it up with the works and make a pot of tea – why not?

Method

1. Check fish for bones. Remove any with tweezers.

2. Spread flour on a plate. Turn fish in it till lightly coated.

3. For crumb: blitz bread, garlic and herbs in processor. Add lemon rind if using. Season. Tip onto plate.

4. Crack egg into shallow bowl with mustard. Beat with fork.

5. Run floured fish through the egg mix. Let it drip a bit. Then lay onto crumb mix and turn to coat both sides.

6. Heat oils in frying pan. Lay fish bits in to sizzle. Reduce heat. Cook for 2–3 minutes till browned. Turn. Fry side two till fish is crisp outside, milk-white and flaky in the middle. Drain on kitchen paper. Serve.

For 2

2 x 175 g/6 oz pieces of firm white fish fillet, skinned (cod loin, haddock)
Plain white flour for coating
2 slices white bread, crusts removed
2 cloves garlic, peeled
Good few sprigs parsley, coriander or dill
Lots of grated lemon rind (optional)
Salt and black pepper
1 egg
1 tsp English mustard
1 tbsp sunflower oil
Little olive oil

Eat with: Mushy peas (chop a bit of fresh mint and squeeze of lemon in for posh), lemon or lime for squeezing, bread'n'butter. Starving? Get some speedy fried spuds in (page 61).

TIME TRICK

Fish cooks faster if cut into fingers.

Mega fast veg

Fact: vegetables are total taste and health gods. They boost your immune system. Sort your hair and skin out. Kick-start your energy. Cook them right and they taste more than right. Team them up with your best mains or slap loads centre stage. I love 'em.

Ingredients
Courgettes
Red or orange peppers
Asparagus
Red onions
Aubergines
Butternut squash
Sweet potato
Olive oil
Sea salt and black
   pepper
Lemon or lime for
   squeezing
Chilli (optional)
Fresh coriander or
   parsley

Eat with:
Shaved Parmesan
Crumbled goats' cheese
or feta
Garlic or harissa mayo
(page 123)
Hummus (page 37)
Salsa verde (page 55)
Guacamole (page 38)
Hey … works with
everything…

Great griddled veg
The best vegetable plate in the world? Could be.
Method
1. Prep veg. **Courgettes:** cut lengthways in thinnish strips or diagonal chunks. **Peppers:** Cut in half or quarters. Ditch seeds, pith, stalk. **Asparagus:** Cut off woody end. **Red onions:** Peel. Cut in chunks. **Aubergines:** Slice thinly across. **Butternut squash and sweet potato:** Peel. Cut in 1 cm/½ in slices.
2. Preheat griddle pan. Tip veg on plate. Brush with very little oil. Slap veg on really hot pan to sizzle till underside is char-grilled. Turn with tongs. Some bits will cook quickly – thick ones will take longer. Remove each veg as it's ready till all are done.
3. Slap veg on plate. Dress with what you will. Bit of olive oil, lime or lemon juice, sea salt, optional finely chopped chilli, chopped fresh herbs. Eat warm or room temperature.

Green beans with tomato & garlic

My brother Tom plays five-a-side on Saturdays, goes food shopping for the week then cooks dinner for his uni mates or his girlfriend. He does his beans this way. Note: if you're cooking freshly picked beans skip the tomato and garlic – just quick boil them.

For 2–3
200 g/7 oz fine green beans, both ends cut off
2 garlic cloves, finely sliced
1 tomato, chopped small
Little olive oil
Sea salt and black pepper

VARIATION
SPEEDY SALAD NIÇOISE
Why not slap on half a tin drained tuna, few black olives, warm boiled egg cut in two.

Method
1. Boil pan of water with bit of salt. Chuck beans in. Cook till just softening. Drain well.
2. Heat a little oil in a frying pan. Throw in the garlic. After a few seconds add tomato then beans. Turn well till heated. Serve.

Speedy fried potatoes

What's scrunchy outside, hot, soft and flaky inside, a bit salty and usually addictive? Try cooking these in duck fat – any excuse to roast duck breast (page 111), just save the fat for this. A great way to use up cold boiled or roast potatoes.

For 2
Cold cooked potatoes, cut in chunks, or 450 g/ 1 lb, cooked fresh (page 62)
1–2 tbsps olive oil or duck fat
Sea salt and black pepper
Parsley, coriander or dill, chopped
Lemon for squeezing

Method
1. Slap duck fat or olive oil to heat in a frying pan that's large enough for all spuds to sit flat.
2. Add spuds when hot. Let edges get good and crusty before turning with palette knife. Bits may flake off but no problem.
3. When hot and golden all over squeeze a bit of lemon, sprinkle herbs and sea salt. Serve.

For 2
350 g/12 oz baby new
  potatoes
Little salt

WHY NOT?
Crush your spuds
with a fork and
drizzle with olive
oil. Or roll in butter
and garlic and
loadsa chopped
parsley. Tasty.

For 2
350 g/12 oz potatoes
Extra virgin olive oil
2 shallots, peeled and
  sliced
Lemon
Sea salt and black
  pepper
Dill, coriander or parsley,
  chopped
1 chorizo sausage, sliced
Dill pickle or pickled
  cucumber, sliced

VARIATION
SMOKED SALMON
At STEP 3 substitute
chorizo with bits of
smoked salmon.

For 2
3 medium tomatoes
1 clove garlic, crushed
Pinch sugar
Olive oil
Salt
Basil leaves (optional)

WHY NOT?
Top each half with
pesto (page 124),
tapenade (page 123)
or grated Parmesan.

Baby potatoes

Easy eaters. Add tasty extras or cook, slice and grill in a dish
with grated cheese, spring onion, sour cream, herbs and
mustard. Note: got more time? Use peeled old spuds. Sort out
floury acts like Maris Piper, King Edward, Desiree.

Method

1. Boil kettle. Put washed spuds in pan with salt. Pour boiling water over.
2. Boil for 10–15 minutes or till soft. Test for doneness with sharp knife.
Drain. Top with plain or herb butter. Salt. Squeeze of lemon.

Top hot potato salad with chorizo

I made this one day when there wasn't much in.
Now it's a regular feature. It works with new baby
spuds. Try with oldies if you've time. A floury
texture means they soak up more flavour.

Method

1. Boil new spuds or old peeled ones (cut in chunks for
speed) for 10–15 minutes or till cooked through. Drain.
2. Throw into bowl. Cut new spuds in two. Chuck shallot
in with herbs, loads of lemon, salt, pepper, drizzle of oil.
Mix gently.
3. While potatoes are cooking, fry chorizo gently in bit of oil
2 minutes each side or till cooked through.
4. Tip chorizo and oil from pan into cooked potato mix.
Throw pickle in. Eat hot, warm or cold.

Hot tomatoes

Tomato salad's cool but sometimes you want
them red hot. For max speed slice across 3 or 4
times and fry a few seconds per side. More time?
You do the main course, the oven does this one.

Method

1. Preheat oven to 230°C/450°F/gas 8. Cut tomatoes in two
across. Spread each half with crushed garlic, bit of sea
salt, sugar, drizzle little olive oil. Top with optional basil leaf.
2. Roast for 10–15 minutes. Add a squeeze of lime or lemon
if you like.

Stir-fried greens

Greens've got a bad name. It's not their fault. Try them the Chinese way. Chuck one or more into a wok. Give them speed, heat, and cool Asian flavours.

Method

1. Wash veg (get rid of trapped soil at base of pak choi, choy sum leaves). Dry to avoid spluttering when frying.

2. Heat a wok or frying pan on medium heat. Add oils to heat.

3. Add garlic. Don't burn. Stir-fry fast to soften, stirring with wooden spoon.

4. Add one or more veg starting with the largest. Stir rapidly to coat and cook. Add a bit of soy.

For 2
Choose one or more from these veg:

Courgettes, cut into bite-size chunks
Mangetout
Pak choi, leaves stripped and sliced
Choy sum, leaves stripped and sliced
Chinese or English cabbage, shredded
Spinach

Groundnut oil plus a little sesame oil
4 cloves garlic, sliced
Soy sauce

VARIATIONS
FRUITY
At STEP 3 add soy, lime juice, pinch of sugar.
CHILLI
At STEP 3 add red chilli and peeled, finely chopped ginger.
ONIONY
At STEP 3 add loadsa chopped spring onion.

15 minutes

Fastest noodles

Noodles are a bit like pasta. They've versatile. Tasty. Brilliant. Slap them into soup. Treat them to a stir-fry. Make noodle cake. (It goes with loads of stuff.) Pack in those oriental flavours. Quality.

For 4
600 ml/1 pint chicken stock or vegetable stock (pg 122) or good quality bought one
6 cloves garlic, halved
1 small piece root ginger, peeled and chopped
1 tbsp soy sauce
110 g/4 oz egg or Japanese soba noodles
225 g/8 oz pak choi
Half 250 g/9 oz pack tofu, chopped in small cubes, and/or handful of cold roast chicken, shredded
2 spring onions, chopped
Fresh basil or coriander

VARIATIONS
DUCK, BEEF, OR PORK NOODLE SOUP
At STEP 4 top with thin slices of cooked duck, beefsteak or pork. Extra flavour? Drizzle my ginger teriyaki (page 53).

 **TIME TRICK**

Use Sunday roast to make chicken stock for this and other post-school dishes. Save some meat for this soup on Monday.

Noodle soup

Paradise in a bowl. Just the smell of it gets me going. Easy to make. Great health boost. Note: sort out own stock or use a good quality bought one.

Method

1. Take two large saucepans. Fill one two-thirds full with water. Put it on the hob to boil. Pour chicken or veg stock into pan two. Add garlic, ginger, chicken if using and soy. Bring to boil then lower to simmer for 10 minutes.

2. Meanwhile, wash and prep veg. Cook noodles (fresh 1 minute, dried 4) in boiling water. Drain. Slap in bowls.

3. Taste stock. Adjust flavours. Add pak choi. Simmer for 3 minutes. Put tofu and chicken in bowls. Pour veg and stock over. Top with herbs and spring onion.

Stir-fry noodles & beansprouts

This is good enough to eat on its own (Chinese-style comfort food) or when you've the time, turn it out as part of a Chinese food banquet.

Method

1. Boil large pan of unsalted water. Stick noodles in. Cook for 4 minutes. Drain. Run under cold water. Mix sauce ingredients.

2. Heat a wok or frying pan. Add oil. When hot stir garlic in. Cook for a few seconds. Add spring onion and ginger. Keep stirring.

3. Slide in cooked noodles and beansprouts. Stir-fry for 2 minutes. Add good squeeze of lime juice, pinch sugar, sauce mix. Cook on for another minute.

For 3
225 g/8 oz thin dried egg noodles
4 cloves garlic, sliced
4 spring onions, chopped, or 2 shallots, finely sliced
Small knob ginger, peeled and grated or chopped
1 tbsp groundnut oil with a bit of sesame oil
225 g/8 oz beansprouts
Pinch sugar
Fresh lime
Bit of fresh coriander, chopped

Sauce
1 tbsp soy sauce
1 tbsp oyster or veggie oyster sauce
1 tbsp sweet chilli sauce

Noodle cake

Simple but brilliant. Think crunchy-style pancake with soft noodle centre. Slice like cake or heap it high with the stuff you're eating. No noodles? Cook cold cooked spaghetti in olive oil.

Method

1. Bring a large pan of unsalted water to boil. Cook noodles for 3–4 minutes. Drain. Run under cold water. Drain again.

2. Tip into bowl and stir through 1 tablespoon oil (bit sesame, rest sunflower).

3. Heat remaining oil in light shallow frying pan. Flatten noodles in like a pancake. Cook 4–5 minutes or till crisp.

4. Very carefully place a large plate or baking tray over pan. Hold firmly together then turn pan over so the cake drops down. Slide noodle cake back into pan. Fry side two till crisp. Slip onto kitchen paper and slice.

For 2–3
225 g/8 oz dried egg noodles
2–3 tbsps sunflower oil
Little sesame oil

Eat with: Sliced steak, sliced duck breast, tuna steak or any meat or vegetable stir-fry.

TIME TRICK

Cook and re-heat noodle cake later in hot oven.

Fastest pasta

Pasta's like a pet. It's good to have about and it's really relaxing. Give it a good boil up in a large pan with loads of water (your pasta, not your pet). Factor water boiling plus pasta cooking time. Use that time to tame yourself some speedy sauces.

For 2
1–2 tbsps olive oil
1 small onion or 2
    shallots, chopped small
2 cloves garlic, crushed
400 g/14 oz can
    chopped tomatoes
Good pinch sugar
1 tbsp tomato purée
Chopped fresh basil,
    parsley or coriander
Salt and black pepper
Squeeze lemon juice
225 g/8 oz pasta
Salt for water
Fresh pesto (page 124)
Parmesan, grated

Eat with: Garlic bread.
Crunchy green salad.

TIME TRICK

Use more sauce for pizza bases.

VARIATIONS
SPICE
At STEP 3 add
pinch cinnamon.
CHEESE
At STEP 5 stir in
small cubes
mozzarella.

Any pasta with tomato sauce & pesto

Tomato's a classic sauce to go with any pasta. If Shakespeare had written sauces, this is the one he'd have made up. Team it up with freshly grated Parmesan, pesto, salad.

Method

1. Put a large saucepan of salted water on high heat to boil. Lid on.
2. Start sauce. Heat oil in pan. Add onion or shallot, garlic and pinch salt. Cook till soft, not brown.
3. Tip in tomatoes, sugar, tomato purée, herbs, pepper, pinch salt, lemon juice. Boil. Reduce heat. Leave to simmer until serving point. Stir occasionally. Add little water if it gets too thick.
4. Add pasta to boiling water. Cover. Boil. Uncover. Stir to stop sticking. Cook till done (see packet). To check, bite a bit. You want it soft, not soggy.
5. Drain pasta. Return to pan. Add a little oil or butter, crushed garlic. Mix.
6. To serve, stick tomato sauce in with pasta. Mix. Slap on plate with pesto and Parmesan on top. Or slap buttered pasta on plate. Run a teaspoon of pesto into a bit of it. Stick tomato sauce on the non-pestoed pasta. Sprinkle Parmesan.

Hot penne with cool tomatoes & olives

Buy one get one free. Eat hot and cold first time round. Get it all chilled as pasta salad later. Good relaxing summer eating. Chuck a load in a box for away-days.

Method

1. Put a large saucepan of salted water on to boil with the lid on.

2. Meantime, throw tomatoes, cucumber, onion, herbs, olives, glug of olive oil, squeeze of lemon juice into a bowl to combine flavours.

3. Put penne into boiling water. Slap lid on pan to re-boil. Uncover. Boil pasta for 10 minutes.

4. Taste piece of pasta for doneness. Drain.

5. Tip penne into large bowl. Throw tomato and olive mix in. Stir. Taste. Drizzle with bit more lemon, oil, herb seasoning if it needs it. Spritz this up when cold with a bit of salad dressing.

For 2

175 g/6 oz dried penne
4 large ripe tomatoes, roughly chopped
Cucumber, peeled and chopped
Bit of red onion, peeled and sliced thin
Black olives, pitted, chopped or whole
Extra virgin olive oil
1 lemon
Fresh herbs of choice parsley, basil, oregano thyme, coriander, mint
Black pepper and sea salt

Eat with: warm crunchy bread to mop up the juices.

15 minutes

VARIATION

THE SHARP ONE
At STEP 5 add good handful croutons, 50 g/2 oz of Roquefort cheese in tiny pieces and a few bits of walnut.

THE BACON ONE
At STEP 5 add 4 fried rashers, crumbled pancetta or streaky bacon, 1 x 400 g/14 oz can of drained, warmed haricot beans and 4 finely chopped spring onions.

Galloping grains

Some of the coolest foods going. And all team players. Couscous is light. It likes to work out with strong flavours. Bulgar wheat tastes a bit nutty. Makes tabbouleh. Customize it. Drizzle and mix with a range of textures and flavours.

For 2
300 ml/½ pint water
225 g/8 oz couscous
Dressing
50 ml/2 fl oz extra virgin
   olive oil
2 tbsps lemon juice
2 tsps red harissa paste
Zest of 1 lemon
2 tbsps parsley or
   coriander, chopped
25 g/1 oz raisins,
   chopped (optional)
25 g/1 oz dried apricot
   finely chopped
   (optional)
Salt and black pepper

Eat with:
Griddled halloumi
Kebabs
Lamb chops and steaks
Char-grilled vegetables
Crumbled feta and salad

WHY NOT?
Slap bite-sized bits of chicken on a hot griddle. Turn till crisp outside, white through. Add salt, lemon. Eat on couscous.

Couscous with harissa dressing

You can get couscous at Yorkshire farmers' markets in huge pans with spicy sauces on top. Do it at home like this with a scorchy harissa. Treat a bland grain to a tasty party.

Method

1. Pour boiling water from kettle into measuring jug. Tip couscous into heatproof bowl. Add water. Stir with fork. Cover with tea towel. Leave for 5 minutes.

2. Meanwhile tip dressing ingredients into another bowl. Mix. Leave.

3. Break soaked couscous up with a fork. Tip onto large plate. Season. Fluff with a fork. Drizzle with dressing. Add any extras. Go party…

Couscous salad

Totally styley. Get a big pile of this on the table. A lean one: good for people with a sweet shop habit.

Method

1. Cook couscous as on previous page. Tip onto large plate. Season. Drizzle with olive oil, fresh lemon juice or sparky dressing. Mix in with fork.

2. Prepare salad veg. Pile on top of couscous. Add more dressing or oil and lemon if you like.

For 2
300 ml/½ pint water
225 g/8 oz couscous
2 fat ripe tomatoes, chopped small
1 red pepper, de-seeded and chopped small
3 spring onions or piece of red onion, chopped small
Black olives, pitted and chopped (optional)
Fresh coriander, parsley or mint, chopped
Extra virgin olive oil
Lemon juice or my sparky dressing (page 122)
Salt and black pepper

Eat with: Griddled steak, tuna, vegetables. Veg and meat kebabs. Roast lamb. Cold roast chicken. Baked or griddled chicken breast.

Tabbouleh

Worth plating up if you're into your weights. Bulgar packs a powerful protein punch. Herbs are full of vits and minerals. They work out together and taste great. A lean eat. Team up with crisp garlic pittas (page 38) or warm flatbreads.

For 2
110 g/4 oz bulgar wheat
600 ml/1 pint water
5–6 tbsps extra virgin olive oil
Juice of 2–3 lemons
Salt and black pepper
Handful mint, chopped
Handful parsley, chopped
3 tomatoes, diced small
1 cucumber, diced small
1 red onion, diced small
Rocket or lettuce (optional)

Method

1. Put water and wheat in a pan. Bring to boil. Cover. Simmer for 10 minutes or till tender. Drain really well. Spread on tea towel or kitchen paper.

2. Meantime, prep other ingredients.

3. Finally, tip dry cooked wheat in a bowl. Mix in oil, lemon juice, seasoning. Add chopped herbs. Mix it.

4. At this point you can add tomatoes, cucumber and onion to the mix. Or slap the herby wheat on a plate. Sit piles of chopped salad round it.

 TIME TRICK

Think ahead. Pour boiling water over bulgar wheat. Soak for 30 minutes. Drain it.

15 minutes

Speedy fruit

Time to get some more fruit down. Sort these three awesome five star puddings.

For 4
Good handful blueberries
Good handful raspberries
Splash orange juice or white wine
25 g/1 oz icing sugar, sifted
4 meringues
300 ml/½ pint double cream

VARIATION
No meringue? Sub in crumbled amaretti or crushed ginger biscuits.

Ingredients
2–3 ripe figs per person
Runny honey

Eat with: Crème fraîche, mascarpone or vanilla and honey ice-cream. Sit on butter-fried slices of sweet brioche.

Eton blueberry mess

Cool. One of those recipes where exact quantities don't matter. Get the balance of fruit just as you like.

Method
1. Throw half the fruit whole in a bowl. Mash rest with a fork to release the juices.
2. Splash juice or wine to soak fruit. Add icing sugar. Chill for 10 minutes.
3. Crush meringues. Whip cream till holding its shape, but not grainy.
4. Gently fold meringues, cream and fruit into tumblers or bowls. Enjoy it.

Hot sticky figs

Figs are small and perfectly formed. Buy ripe. (Figs stop maturing when picked.) Get untorn skins. Peel banana style using your fingers. For fig formal slice up with Parma ham, salty cheese and your best salad. For sweet and simple, honey whole-roast them.

Method
1. Preheat oven to 190°C/375°F/gas 5.
2. Drizzle a bit of water over a baking tray. Sit figs on top. Stick in the oven for 10 minutes.
3. Remove. Leave to cool for a minute. Cut a cross into figs to splay open a bit. Drizzle honey into each. Slap back into oven for 4–5 minutes.

Raspberry ginger cream pancakes

A cracking pud. Impress a special friend (or treat yourself – why not). Crisp pancake. Sherbety ginger cream. Cool raspberries.

Method

1. Filling: Tip cream in bowl. Beat with rotary hand whisk till soft and holding shape – not stiff. Gently stir in sugar and ginger. Add raspberries.

2. Pancakes: Sift flour and salt into bowl. Dent flour. Crack egg in. Add glug of milk or milk and water from measuring jug. Whisk with balloon whisk or wooden spoon using circular wrist action, adding rest of milk bit by bit, for a smooth lump-free batter. Pour into measuring jug.

3. Heat non-stick crêpe, pancake or frying pan. Slap in a bit of butter to sizzle. Pancakes need heat but don't burn the butter. Brush butter over pan surface or swirl it.

4. Put 2–3 tablespoons of batter in pan. Pour from jug if you can judge it. Swirl pan using circular wrist action to coat surface. Cook till underside browned, top bubbled. Toss or use palette knife to flip it. Cook other side. (First pancake often sticks. Chuck it away. The next one'll work.)

5. Lay pancake on warm plate. Spoon cream filling down one side. Roll to wrap it up. Drizzle with maple syrup. Good squeeze of lemon juice. Note: save any extra pancakes for re-heating later.

Makes 8 pancakes
110 g/4 oz plain flour
Pinch salt
1 egg
300 ml/½ pint milk or
   half milk, half water
Butter for frying

Filling
200 ml/7 fl oz double
   cream
1 tbsp caster sugar
2 tsps ground ginger
225 g/8 oz fresh
   raspberries
Maple syrup and lemon
   or lime juice for drizzling
Icing sugar for dusting

TIME TRICK

Batter's speedy but make it ahead. It'll sit in the fridge for hours. Re-whisk it.

15 minutes

20 minutes
Enjoy

You're sitting in a field, knackered. Tent leaks. What d'you need? Twenty minutes and a sausage.

Cooking hints get basic here. Beans. Eggs. Brilliant stuff. Love it. Love burgers so long as they're the real thing. Get everyone back and dry and stack some.

20 minutes is just about time for a dinner party. Invite a good mate, a couple of ladies round. Candles on the table. Pasta works. I keep mashes to myself. I'm lying. All my mates have got a favourite. Mozzarella stacks work for girls. Get the biscuits out with my lush plum pudding.

Belting burgers

Saturday means footie at the local ground and a good pie. Back with my mates for PS2 and home-style burger. Real burgers sort you out. Made with real meat they're damned good for you. Blitz the basics before you go out. Cook and stack soon as you're back. Note: you could work from scratch using mates as sous-chefs.

For 4
50 g/2 oz bread, no crusts
4 spring onions
2 cloves garlic
450 g/1 lb chicken breasts
1 red chilli
4 tbsps chopped, fresh coriander
Grated rind of 1 lemon or 2 limes
Few drops soy sauce
Little sunflower and sesame oil

To stack:
4 bread buns
Fresh lime juice
Garlic mayo (page 123)
Sweet chilli sauce
Sushi ginger
Rocket or lettuce

WHY NOT?
Make spritzy salad. Blanch beansprouts in boiling water for 1 minute. Cool under tap. Drain. Mix with sliced red pepper, spring onions, chopped coriander in a bowl with a good drizzle of ginger teriyaki (page 53) or my sparky dressing (page 122).

Thai-style chicken burger

Go Thai-style with this cool chicken. It's great as a burger but you could do it small-style as Thai-cakes. Dip in teriyaki or lime ginger drizzle for gatherings and chopstick eating.

Method

1. Preheat oven to 200°C/400°F/gas 6. Tip bread, spring onion, garlic into processor. Blitz.
2. Roughly chop chicken and chilli then add to mix. Blitz. (Don't overdo it. You want mince, not pulp.) Blitz briefly again with coriander.
3. Mix in lime or lemon rind, few drops of soy. Make mix into 4 flattened burger shapes by hand (or make 4 small burgers and freeze the rest).
4. Put oil to heat in pan. Fry each side 2 minutes to colour.
5. Finish in oven for 10 minutes or till cooked through. Or cook in pan till done.
6. Stick burger in a warmed bun with squeeze of lime juice, garlic mayo, bit of chilli sauce, bit of sushi ginger, rocket or lettuce.

Brilliant beefburger – the real McCoy

Keep these plain meaty. Or jazz them up. You choose. Buy best minced steak from your butcher or blitz your own. My mate Fordy reckons this is the best meal he's eaten in his life. Girls I know who hate burgers eat this and fall in love – with burgers.

VARIATION
CHEESE AND BACON BURGER
At STEP 6 grill four rashers smoked back bacon. Flash grill slices of Cheddar on burger. Top with bacon and sliced dill pickle.

Method

1. Heat oil in pan. Add onion, garlic, bit of salt. Fry gently till soft. Cool.
2. Own mince: Cube beef. Stick a few cubes in processor and blitz. Repeat.
3. Slap mince (own or bought) in bowl. Add herbs, egg, ketchup, seasoning, fried onion and garlic.
4. Mix well with fork. Form into 4 burgers. Fridge for 5 minutes.
5. Meantime prep rolls, stacking stuff and relishes.
6. Preheat griddle, frying pan or grill. Brush burgers with a little oil. Cook 3 minutes each side. Repeat till cooked to taste – medium rare (for good meat) or well done. Timing depends on thickness of burger. Rest for 1 minute. Stack them.
Basic stack: 1. Warmed, griddled or toasted roll. **2.** Burger. **3.** Sliced tomato **4.** Rocket or lettuce **5.** Tomato sauce, guacamole, sweet chilli sauce, mayo.

For 4
Little olive oil
1 medium onion, finely chopped
2 cloves garlic, crushed
450 g/1 lb beef for mincing (rump's good) or best steak mince
Few sprigs of fresh thyme or 3 tbsps chopped fresh parsley
1 small egg, beaten
1 tsp tomato ketchup
Salt and black pepper
4 soft baps

For 2
2 chicken breasts,
  bashed a bit to flatten
Salt and black pepper
Olive oil

Marinade
200 ml/7 oz natural
  yogurt
2 tsps brown sugar
3 cloves garlic, crushed
1 tsp cumin
1 tsp coriander
Flat parsley, finely
  chopped
Good squeeze lemon
  juice

WHY NOT?
Team with fruit
salsa. Chop mango
or pineapple with a
bit of diced red
onion, a red chilli,
de-seeded and finely
sliced, finely
chopped mint or
coriander, a bit of
caster sugar, olive
oil. Mix. Awesome.

For 4
50 g/2 oz white bread,
  crust-free
450 g/1 lb pork steak or
  best minced pork
50 g/2 oz apple, grated
1 medium onion, finely
  chopped
Rind of 1 lemon
Good few gratings
  peeled, fresh ginger
Loads of fresh coriander,
  finely chopped
Salt and black pepper
1 small egg

Eat with: Sour cream,
honey and mustard
dressing or coleslaw.

Whole piece chicken sugar burger

It's called a burger but it's not mashed like a burger. It's bashed up to flatten it. Stick in your bun. Stack with the usuals. It's sweet. Lean. Delicious.

Method

1. Preheat oven to 200°C/400°F/gas 6. Mix all marinade ingredients in bowl.
2. If chicken breasts are thin, leave them. Slap thick ones between clingfilm or greaseproof paper. Flatten a bit with a rolling pin. Chuck chicken in marinade. Leave for 5 minutes.
3. Oil griddle lightly. Heat well. Pick chicken up letting excess mix drop off. Season it with salt and black pepper. Sizzle 4 minutes each side.
4. Stick on baking tray in oven for 5–10 minutes or till white all through. Test with skewer or sharp knife. Should be a bit springy.
5. Rest for 1 minute. Stack in bun or griddled flat bread with cucumber, mayo or garlic yogurt, green leaf. Eat with sweet potato chips and mustard mayo.

Pork burger

Dim sum fans will really go for these. Don't panic if they break up a bit. (They must glue commercial burgers together.) You can pan-fry but I like to grill them. Note: I add loadsa ginger. My top burger.

Method

1. Blitz bread to crumbs in processor. Or grate it. Chuck in large bowl.
2. Own mince: Cut pork into cubes. Tip a few in processor. Blitz a few seconds till minced (not pulped!). Repeat till all done.
3. Own or bought mince: Slap in bowl with apple, onion, lemon rind, ginger, coriander, salt, lots of black pepper. Mix well with fork. Beat egg. Add just enough to bind mix together. Don't get it too wet. Get your hands in to make burger shapes. Fridge for 5 minutes.
4. Preheat grill. Line pan with foil. Grill burgers 5 minutes each side or till cooked right through. Stack.

Falafel burger

All-year Glastonbury-style eating. My veggie and vegan sisters go for this. Eat in rolls or pitta with extras or sit it on streetwise salads. Note 1: enough protein in here to keep you going through all-night gig (I wish). Note 2: get chickpeas dry so falafels don't dematerialize when frying.

Method

1. Drain chickpeas well. Spread on kitchen paper. Roll to dry.
2. Blitz bread to crumbs in processor or grate (use stale bread). Add chickpeas, onion, garlic, spices, herbs, salt and black pepper. Blitz to a paste that'll stick together.

3. Tip mix onto big plate or board. Take table-spoonfuls. Make flattish shapes (small burgers). Roll lightly in flour (helps stop falafel dissolving). Fridge for a few minutes if you have time.
4. Pour oil in smallish pan till 1 cm/½ in deep. Heat. Shallow fry falafel gently for 2–3 minutes till lightly browned. Turn very gently. Fry till coloured and cooked through. Stack in buns with salad, on leaves, or stuff in warm pittas.

For 2–3
1 x 400 g/14 oz can chickpeas
50 g/2 oz white bread
1 medium onion, roughly chopped
5 cloves garlic, peeled
2 tsps ground coriander
2 tsps ground cumin
1 tsp chilli powder
2 tbsps coriander, chopped
Salt and black pepper
2 tbsps white flour for rolling
Sunflower or groundnut oil for frying

Eat with: Tomato and red onion salad, olives, garlic, yogurt, cucumber, hummus (page 37) or guacamole (page 38).

20 minutes

Campfire eggs & other stuff

Ah the great outdoors. A load of hills, manky cows, loadsa rain, leaky tent, no sleep, snoring mates. But there's always the cooking. Everything tastes better, sharper. Stuff to take? Camping stove, mug, plate, wooden spoon, spoon, fork, knife, tin opener, mess tin for cooking and eating.

Per person
Water
Teabag
2 good quality sausages
1 rasher good rindless
  bacon
1 egg
200 g/7 oz tin baked
  beans
1–2 slices bread
Little olive oil

Trekking breakfast – a sausage fry-up

Get a head start. Get a full fry-up down before you set off in the morning. Your mates'll love you. Top tips: 1. Don't cook in your tent (even the porch). It's a tent not a beacon. 2. Boil water for a nice cup of tea before you start cooking. 3. Metal forks burn. Use a wooden fork or spoon for cooking. 4. Timing's everything. Do it in order.

Method

1. Put stove on level ground. Light it. Boil water for tea in mess tin. Pour over tea bag. Add milk and sugar if you like/have any. Tip away excess water.
2. Turn heat down. Pour tiny bit of oil in mess tin. Slap bangers in. Keep turning as you slow fry to cook through. Could take 15–20 minutes depending on thickness of sausage.
3. When nearly cooked, slap bacon rashers in. Cook first side then turn.
4. Plate sausage and bacon or stick between bread. Turn heat up. Crack egg into pan. Fry. Flick oil over yolk to set it. Plate it.
5. Tip beans in pan. Heat. Stirring. Eat it.

Eggs in the nest

Sorts you out when you're totally knackered and your brain's scrambled so you want something fast, calming. Maybe better not let the birds see. Note: don't scramble eggs camping. Washing it off the pan's a total nightmare.

Per person
2 slices bread
2 medium eggs
2 tsps fat or olive oil

Method

1. Put a bit of oil to heat in mess tin.
2. Cut a hole in middle of each slice of bread. Approx 6 cm/2½ in.
3. Fry side one till crispy. Turn with fork and wooden spoon.
4. Crack egg in hole. Reduce heat. Cover tin. Cook 3 minutes or till done.

Camping pasta with tomato or tuna'n'tomato sauce

Bold. Maybe try it out at home first if you're a novice. You'll need two pans for this one.

Method

1. Put pan of water on stove to boil. Slip pasta in. Boil up for 4 minutes.

2. Take pasta pan off stove. Cover. Leave for pasta to cook slowly in water.

3. Turn flame down a bit. Put oil to heat in other pan. Tip in onions, garlic, bit of salt. Stir with wooden spoon till soft, not browned.

4. Take onion pan off stove. Put pasta pan to boil up again for a minute. Remove from stove.

5. Put onion pan back. Tip in tomatoes (and tuna if using). Break tuna to bits with fork. Simmer till sauce heats up well and comes together.

6. Check pasta is done. Put it back to boil if you need, keeping tomato sauce covered. Drain pasta, top with sauce and plate it. Bit of grated cheese would be nice.

For 2
225 g/8 oz fusilli pasta
1 litre/1¾ pints water
Pinch salt
1 medium onion, peeled finely chopped
1 clove garlic, finely sliced
2 tsps olive oil
400 g/14 oz tin chopped tomatoes
200 g/7 oz tin tuna, drained (optional)

20 minutes

Relax with pasta

You'll be laughing with these. Every sauce has a mood and a pasta that goes with it. Pasta's popular with mates. It's a good filler. It sorts you right out. (Use the carbs for training. They'll keep you going. Weirdly enough they also relax you.) Could you ask for more? I don't think so. Note: always cook pasta in loadsa water.

For 4
25 g/1 oz butter
1 tbsp olive oil
1–2 rashers back bacon,
  chopped small
1 onion, chopped small
2 cloves garlic, crushed
450 g/1 lb beef mince
400 g/14 oz can
  chopped tomatoes
3 tbsps tomato purée
Good pinch of sugar
Fresh parsley, oregano
  or thyme
1 bay leaf
Little grated nutmeg
150 ml/5 fl oz red wine,
  stock or water
Lemon juice
Salt and black pepper
350 g/12 oz spaghetti
Parmesan for sprinkling

Eat with: Garlic bread

Cheeky spaghetti Bolognese

A classic pasta in just 20 minutes. How good is that? Use great meat. Spices punch in the flavour. Note: give the sauce extra time if you can blag it. Or make it the day before and re-heat.

Method

1. Sauce: Melt butter and oil in large pan. Add bacon. Stir with wooden spoon for 1 minute. Add onion, garlic. Cook gently till soft, not brown.
2. Raise heat. Add beef. Whack it round till all browned.
3. Tip in red wine to bubble for 1 minute. Add tomatoes, purée, sugar, herbs, bay leaf, nutmeg, seasoning.
4. Bubble it. Put lid on. Reduce heat. Simmer. Check and stir. Add bit of water if it gets dry or tomato purée to thicken it.
5. Spaghetti: Meantime boil large pan salted water. Add pasta. Cover. Boil. Uncover. Cook 10 minutes or till done. Bite a bit to test. Should be just soft. Drain. Throw it back into pan. Add bit extra olive oil or butter if you like.
6. Squeeze bit of lemon into sauce. Stir and taste – add more if you like. Adjust seasoning. Tip sauce in with pasta. Mix well. Serve. Or slap it on top of your plated pasta. Top with Parmesan. Where's the salad?

Sausage & mustard creamy pasta

What it says on the tin. Simple. Delicious. No sweat to make. Don't train till later. You might fall over. (Rule: read the label. Get real meat or good veggie sausages.)

For 2
4 best pork sausages
175 g/6 oz penne
10 g/½ oz butter
150 ml/5 fl oz cream
Salt and black pepper
2 tsps mustard
75 g/2–3 oz freshly grated Parmesan
Few leaves sage, finely chopped (optional)

Method

1. Preheat oven to 220°C/425°F/gas 7. Put sausages on baking tray. Cook for 15–20 minutes.
2. Meantime heat large pan of salted water. Boil up. Cook penne for 8–10 minutes. Test for doneness. Needs to be just soft.
3. Remove sausages from oven. Slice them up.
4. Drain pasta. Slap butter in warm pan to melt. Add cream. Season.
5. Add mustard, pasta, Parmesan, sage and sausage. Mix. Eat with a heap of crispy salad and sparky dressing.

VARIATION
Use chorizo sausage. Slice and fry each side for 3 minutes.

Best courgette herb cream pasta

Comfort food. With a healthy edge. Griddling courgettes means they stay crunchy. Share with a DVD and mates on the sofa.

For 2–4
2 large courgettes, cut across in discs
Sprinkle dried oregano
350 g/12 oz tagliatelle or pappardelle
1 large egg
110 g/4 oz ricotta cheese
4 tbsps grated Parmesan
125 ml/4 fl oz cream
Salt and black pepper
2–3 tbsps parsley, tarragon, basil or dill, finely chopped
Extra Parmesan for sprinkling

Method

1. Heat griddle pan. Brush courgette discs with bit of oil. Slap on griddle. Sizzle to char-grill. Turn. Get them brown but still crisp. Slap on kitchen paper. Sprinkle with bit of dried oregano.
2. Put large pan salted water on to boil for pasta.
3. Start sauce. Crack and separate egg. Tip yolk into bowl. Add ricotta. Mix.
4. Slap pasta into water. Boil for 10 minutes.
5. Finish sauce. Tip cream into small pan with Parmesan, rocket or parsley, salt and black pepper, stirring with wooden spoon. Add ricotta mix. Take off soon as hot. Watch not to burn it.
6. Drain pasta when ready. Tip back into pan. Tip sauce in with herbs, courgettes. Mix. Serve with extra cheese, crunchy chicory or lettuce with balsamic dressing and croutons. Warm crusty or garlic bread.

Save time & bake it

Baking's good. You put a load of stuff in the oven. It does the work. Shame it doesn't do maths, chemistry etc. (OK it does chemistry.) Enjoy yourself with these cool options.

For 2
2 tbsps olive oil
1 large onion, chopped small
1 red pepper, de-seeded and finely chopped
3 cloves garlic, crushed
1–2 chillies, de-seeded, finely chopped
400 g/14 oz tin chopped tomatoes
3 fresh tomatoes, chopped
400 g/14 oz can red kidney beans
2 tbsps tomato purée
Pinch sugar
2 tbsps fresh coriander
Salt and black pepper
4 eggs
2 tortillas

Extras
Grated Cheddar
Sour cream
Chopped avocado
Lime quarters
Warmed tortillas (pg 100)

TIME TRICK

Cover the eggs as they bake – they set a bit faster.

Huevos rancheros
We don't get many Mexican cowboys in our bit of Yorkshire. So we eat these. Eggs baked on a really cool hot chilli pepper tomato salsa. Eat neatly on a plate with warm tortilla (page 100) and extras. Or slap the mix in tortillas with fried eggs. Top with sour cream, cheese, guacamole (page 38). Wrap it.

Method
1. Preheat oven to 200°C/400°F/gas 6.
2. Heat oil in medium saucepan. Add onion, red pepper, pinch of salt. Cook for 2 minutes. Add garlic and chilli. Cook for 1 minute. Add tomatoes, tomato purée, beans, sugar, half the fresh coriander. Boil up. Reduce heat. Simmer for a few minutes till pulpy. Season with little salt and black pepper.
3. Lightly oil shallow baking dish. Spread hot mix across to fill it. Make dents with large spoon. Break egg into each. Slap into oven for 10 minutes or till eggs are set.
4. Meantime prepare extras on large plate for sharing.
5. Scoop spoonfuls onto plates. Top with remaining coriander.

Tomozzarella & auberfeta stacks

Veggie sisters have their uses. You can eat their stuff. Shame they can't have your stuff. Leave the Parma ham off if you're feeling generous. Note: a couple of really styley light eats. One usually falls over.

Method

1. Preheat oven to 200°C/400°F/gas 6.

2. Auberfeta: Cut aubergine in 1 cm/½ in slices. Fry 2 minutes each side or till just soft in little olive oil.

3. Slap first slice down. Layer tomato, feta, aubergine. Repeat. Stick on baking tray. Drizzle with little oil.

4. Tomozzarella: Slice tomatoes across into four or five. Sit bottom slice on baking tray. Smear with pesto. Cover with mozzarella. Layer with optional basil leaf; next tomato slice; pesto. Repeat layers till done. Drizzle with little oil. Wrap 1 ham slice round tomato. Repeat with second tomato.

5. Bake 10–15 minutes.

For 2
Auberfeta
1 aubergine
Olive oil
2 large tomatoes, sliced
Feta, crumbled, from
  200 g/7 oz pack
Tomozzarella
2 large tomatoes
Mozzarella from 150 g/
  5½ oz pack
Pesto
Few basil leaves
Olive oil
2 slices Parma ham

WHY NOT?
Stuff'n'bake tomatoes. Preheat oven as above. Slice tops off tomatoes. Scoop insides out with teaspoon. Drain. Stuff with spare Bolognese, cold cooked rice and grated cheese, or cold cooked rice, grated cheese, raisins, sliced spring onion. Put top back on. Bake 15 minutes.

20 minutes

Comfort mash

Great mash is a bit like a duvet. Warm, comfortable, never lumpy.
Fast mash guidance: 1. Use floury spuds (Maris Piper, King
Edward). 2. Sort lumps with a fork, a masher, a ricer or a whisk.
3. Add tasty smoothers like milk, butter, cream, egg, olive oil,
herbs, mustard, cheese, lemon
juice, spring onion and garlic.

For 4
900 g/2 lb potatoes
  peeled, cut in chunks
50 g/2 oz butter
125 ml/4 fl oz milk
Salt and black pepper

WHY NOT?
Make great
bubble'n'squeak.
Take cold or fresh
mash. Add half
again chopped fresh
cabbage. Add salt,
black pepper, bit of
beaten egg. Add
grated cheese,
spring onion, cubed
cold meat if you
like. Mould mix into
burger shapes. Coat
in seasoned flour.
Fry 4 minutes each
side in oil till hot
and golden. Eat with
cold roasts, eggs,
gammon, beans,
salad.

Smooth everyday mash

Stick a bowl of this
out, it's like a homing
device. Everyone
knows it's on the
table.

Method
1. Half fill a large pan with
water. Add pinch of salt.
Put on full heat.
2. Slip spuds into water
when prepped. Cover.
Boil 15 minutes or till
done. A sharp knife
should pass through.
Drain in colander.
3. Tip spuds back into
pan on heat for 1 minute
to dry. Jiggle pan so they
don't burn.

4. Heat milk in small pan till very hot.
5. Mash spuds with masher, fork or ricer till lump-free. Add butter. Beat
with wooden spoon. Add milk, gradually, beating as you go. Tip in any
extras like mustard, lemon juice, grated nutmeg, herbs (dill, coriander,
parsley). Mix, season and taste. Sit it in warm oven if mains not ready.

Cheese'n'onion mash

This could be my top mash. It's chic yet cheesy. Share it with your favourite people. Or get a bowl for yourself. Gruyère's cool to use. Cheddar works too. Quality.

Method

1. Put saucepan of water, pinch salt on to fast boil while prepping.

2. Put even-sized chunks of potato into water with garlic. Boil furiously for approximately 15 minutes.

3. Drain spuds when cooked. Test with knife or skewer.

4 Slap spuds back in pan for 1–2 minutes to dry a bit. Don't burn them. Shift about with wooden spoon.

5. Slap butter in. Bash with masher to get lumps out and get it smooth.

6. Add milk. Mix with wooden spoon. Slap cheese in and whack it round over heat so it melts together. Chuck spring onion in at last minute with salt, black pepper. Delicious.

For 2

450 g/1 lb potatoes, peeled and cut in chunks
2 cloves garlic, peeled
25 g/1 oz butter
2 tbsps milk
110 g/4 oz Gruyère cheese
2 spring onions, finely chopped
Salt and black pepper

WHY NOT?

Slap mash on top of Bolognese sauce (page 80). Bake in hot oven for 20 minutes or till hot and bubbling.

Sweet potato mash

Sweet, simple, styley. Go try – the honey and ginger just lifts it.

Method

1. Put saucepan of water to boil with pinch salt while prepping.

2. Put sweet potato into water with grated ginger. Boil furiously for 10–15 minutes.

3. Drain in sieve. Slap back into warm pan to dry for a few seconds.

4. Bash down into lump-free purée with masher. Add a bit of butter and honey, seasoning. Taste. Adjust flavour. Add a little lemon juice or serve wedges for squeezing at table.

For 2

450 g/1 lb sweet potatoes, peeled and cut in large chunks
Few gratings of peeled fresh ginger
Butter
1 tsp runny honey
Salt and black pepper
Squeeze of lemon

Eat with: Gammon, pork, chicken or veggie casserole

20 minutes

Slap up stir-fries

No more scuzzy take-aways and all-you-can-eat buffets. Get these stir-fry classics down and you're totally sorted. Time trick: always prep your ingredients and sauces before you start to stir-fry.

For 4
3 cakes medium egg noodles
60 ml/2 fl oz soy sauce
5 cm/2 in piece fresh ginger, peeled and grated
1 tsp sugar
6 spring onions, trimmed and sliced
Handful beansprouts
1 small onion, sliced
Handful mangetout
12 cooked peeled prawns
3 cloves garlic, sliced
1 chilli, de-seeded and finely sliced
2 chicken breasts, cut in thin strips
Fresh coriander, chopped
2 tbsps sunflower oil
1 tsp sesame oil
2 eggs
Pickled ginger (optional)

VARIATIONS
GAMMON
At STEP 2 sub chunks home-cooked gammon for prawns.
MUSHROOM AND TOFU STIR-FRY
Replace the meat and fish with 250 g/ 9 oz pack tofu and 250 g/9 oz mushrooms.

Prawn & chicken stir-fry

People? Some you like. Others you don't. Food's the same. Prawns and chicken love each other.

Method

1. Bring large saucepan of water to boil. Slap noodles in. Cook for 4 minutes. Drain.
2. Meantime stick soy, ginger, sugar into large bowl. Tip in prawns, noodles, beansprouts, onion, spring onions, mangetout.
3. Beat eggs in small bowl. Add half coriander.
4. Heat wok or frying pan. Add oil. Add garlic, chilli. Stir round fast with care. Add chicken. Stir again for 2–3 minutes.
5. Add contents of large bowl. Stir-fry for 4 minutes, checking everything gets hot.
6. Add egg. Stir-fry for 1 minute. Plate or bowl it. Top with rest of coriander, pickled ginger. Serve with lime wedges.

Lettuce wrapped lamb'n'mushroom stir-fry

Check it out. Fill crisp lettuce leaves with a bit of hoisin sauce, spring onion, cucumber. Top with cool lamb and mushroom stir-fry (or beef if you like). It's not just the taste, it's the cool ritual.

Method

1. Slice base, peel leaves off lettuce for wraps. Slap on plate with cucumber, spring onion sticks. Fridge it.

2. Prep stir-fry: garlic, chilli, mushrooms, spring onion, corriander, cucumber.

3. Heat wok or frying pan. Add oils. When really hot add garlic, chilli. Stir with long-handled spoon to soften for few seconds.

4. Slap mushrooms in. Turn and stir for 3 minutes.

5. Tip in rice wine, sugar, dash of soy, pepper. Stir-fry for 4 minutes or till mushroom mix dry.

6. Chuck mince in. Whack round for 3–4 minutes till cooked and brown. Stir in spring onion, coriander and cucumber bits. Slap wrap bits and hoisin sauce on table. Stick stir-fry in pot. Everyone get wrapping. Drink green tea. Ohm.

For 4

Lettuce wrap
1 iceberg lettuce, chilled
4 tbsps hoisin sauce
Half cucumber, peeled and cut in matchsticks
4 spring onions, cut into matchsticks

Stir-fry
5 cloves garlic, chopped
450 g/1 lb chestnut mushrooms, chopped
1 green chilli, de-seeded and chopped
6 spring onions, chopped
Fresh coriander, chopped
2.5 cm/1 in cucumber, cut into fine chunks
1 tbsp sunflower oil
1 tsp sesame oil
225 g/8 oz minced lamb
1 tbsp rice wine
Little soy sauce
Black pepper
1–2 tsps sugar

20 minutes

Sweet treats

How totally cool and delicious are these?
You won't know till you make 'em.

For 4
Fruit
240 ml/8 fl oz water
110 g/4 oz caster sugar
450 g/1 lb plums
1 tsp rosewater
1 vanilla pod
1 small sprig rosemary

Custard
300 ml/10 fl oz milk
1 vanilla pod or
  few drops essence
  or strip of lemon peel
3 eggs
10 g/$\frac{1}{2}$ oz sugar
5 g/$\frac{1}{4}$ oz cornflour

Bedhead Turkish Delight plums & custard

Chuck herbs and rosewater in with plums and you've got one of the coolest puddings you could dream up. OK they look a bit rough round the edges (bit like me in the mornings). That's part of their style. Sort them out with cinnamon toast fingers (page 21) and great custard.

Method

1. Fruit: Heat water and sugar in medium pan till sugar is dissolved.
2. Add plums, rosewater, vanilla pod (split with knife down middle), rosemary. Simmer very gently for 10–15 minutes or till skins split and plums tenderize. Don't overcook.
3. Custard: Heat milk in medium saucepan with split vanilla pod or essence or lemon. When it just boils, remove (watch it doesn't boil over). Take pod out.
4. Separate eggs. Slap yolks in large bowl with sugar, cornflour. Mix well.
5. Tip hot milk slowly onto mix while stirring with wooden spoon. Tip back in pan.
6. Stir over low heat till thickish. Don't boil. It'll curdle. Stir like mad with pan in cold water if gets grainy. Pour into jug. Eat hot, cold or warm.

Makes 12
110g/4oz oats
10g/$\frac{1}{2}$ oz semolina
75g/3oz soft brown
  sugar
110g/4oz butter

Fast-track flapjacks

Doubt it could be easier or speedier. These are thin, quick. Keep some in your schoolbag or kitbag.

Method

1. Preheat oven to 190°C/375°F/gas 5.
2. Melt butter in pan. Slap oats, semolina, sugar into big bowl.
3. Pour butter into oat mix. Mix well.
4. Tip mix into well greased shallow baking tin, 28 x 18 cm/11 x 7 ins.
5. Press to cover tin. Bake 15 minutes. When slightly cooled, cut into 12 squares with a sharp knife. Leave in tin to cool completely. Remove with care and spatula.

Top chocolate biscuits

Are you a plain, milk or white chocolate biscuit fan? You hate chocolate? Right – ice them.

Method

1. Preheat oven to 190°C/ 375°F/gas 5.

2. Process biscuit ingredients or use mixer. Or by hand: whack butter and sugar into large bowl. Cream till light with wooden spoon. Gradually tip egg in, beating well as you go. Add vanilla.

3. Sift flour in. Add semolina. Mix. Bring smooth dough together with your fingers.

4. Sit dough on lightly floured board. Roll out thinly (3 mm). Cut out with cutter or floured wine glass. Sit on lightly greased baking tray. Bake 10 minutes or till just coloured. Cool on tin for 3 minutes then spatula onto rack. Top when cold (allow another 5 minutes).

Choc top: Melt bits of favourite choc in heatproof bowl over pan of simmering water or microwave. Drop and swirl over tops with a teaspoon.

Ice top: Mix sifted icing sugar with little lemon juice for stiff mix. Spoon and swirl over biscuits.

Makes 10

110 g/4 oz soft butter
110 g/4 oz caster sugar
1 medium egg, well beaten
5 drops vanilla essence
250 g/9 oz plain white flour
25 g/1 oz semolina

Choc top

200 g/7 oz good quality chocolate

Ice top

200 g/7 oz icing sugar
Lemon juice

Orange almond neat biscuits

Stick a small one on your gran's saucer. She'll love you. Coursework due? Schmooze a teacher.

Method

1. Preheat oven to 180°C/350°F/gas 4.

2. Slap first five ingredients in food mixer. Slow mix for fast dough.

3. Or tip butter in a large bowl. Cream with wooden spoon. Add sugar. Cream till soft. Sift in flour. Add almonds and rind. Mix with metal spoon.

4. Pull mix into soft dough ball with fingers. **Small biscuits:** roll bits of dough into hazlenut-sized balls. **Bigger:** roll into walnut-sized balls.

5. Sit biscuits well apart on ungreased baking trays. Flatten a bit with fingers or roll fork across to pattern. Stick jam or cherry in top or leave plain. Bake 10–15 minutes or just colouring. Sprinkle plain with sugar. Cool on tray.

Makes 10–20

110 g/4 oz soft butter
50 g /2 oz caster sugar
110 g/4 oz self-raising flour
25 g/1 oz ground almonds
Grated rind of 1/2 orange
Few glacé cherries, halved (optional)
Bit of red jam (optional)
Extra sugar for sprinkling

20 minutes

30 minutes Sorted

Cooking's a bit like filling your iPod. You want a load of different tunes in there. Hip hop. Soul. Bit of jazz next to your garage. That's this last section. A mix of cool, everyday stuff and some real classics. Stuff for mates, gatherings, family meals. Really cool puds like brandy snap baskets.

OK a couple of these push the boundaries time-wise (they'll tell you who they are), so don't plan to rush for the bus. Just enjoy yourself.

Rules? Well the more relaxed you are, the better the food turns out (my experience). First timer? Been up all night? Be easy on yourself. Could take 30 minutes to get across the kitchen on a bad day. But take all the time you need. Hey – it's the quality of the eating that matters.

Soup

My top two. Everything you want in a bowl. For complete meals team with bread, cheese, fruit, a bit of cool salad.

For 4–6
1–2 tbsps olive oil
3 rashers bacon, chopped
1 large onion, finely chopped
2 cloves garlic, crushed
1 potato, peeled and chopped small
1 carrot, peeled and sliced small
200 g/7 oz red lentils
2 x 400 g/14 oz cans chopped tomatoes
1½ litres/2½ pints chicken or veg stock, or water
1–2 tbsps tomato purée
Pinch sugar
1–2 tbsps parsley, chopped
Salt and black pepper

Eat with: Grated Cheddar, Parmesan or Gruyère. Good warm crusty bread, toasted wholemeal fingers.

VARIATION
RAPID MINESTRONE
At STEP 4 replace lentils with can of cannellini beans. At STEP 5 add handful of broken bits of pasta. Don't blitz it.

Tomato & lentil soup

This one's total tomato pleasure. Good to warm yourself up after sport or lousy weather. Good if you're feeling like rubbish. Good for anything really. Blitz it up for smooth or leave it chunky. Note: vegetarians skip the bacon.

Method

1. Tip oil into large pan. Slap bacon in. Sizzle gently, stirring for 2 minutes.
2. Slap in onion, garlic. Cook till soft, not brown. Add potato, carrot. Put lid on.
3. Sweat veg for few minutes. Meantime put lentils in sieve under tap to wash. Drain.
4. Slap lentils in pan. Add tomatoes, stock, 1 tablespoon purée, half the parsley, sugar, seasoning.
5. Simmer 15–20 minutes with lid on till veg dead soft. Add rest of purée, parsley. Stir. Remove from heat.
6. Taste, adjust seasoning. Serve chunky. For smooth soup, leave 2 minutes. Blitz. Add extra water if too thick, tomato purée if too thin. Re-heat.

VARIATION
COURGETTE AND CHEESE
At STEP 1 chunk chop 450 g/1 lb courgettes in a pan with bit of garlic. Cook gently with butter and garlic for 20 minutes. Meantime cook other ingredients, minus watercress, in another pan. At STEP 6 add ¾ of courgettes to soup. Add basil. Blitz. Stir in rest of courgette, mustard, cheese and lemon juice.

Cheese & watercress soup

Watercress. It's great for skin, hair, bones, brain, energy, immune system, soup. Loves cheese. Quality!

Method

1. Roughly chop watercress. Remove odd tough stalk. Slice leek thinly across. Peel potatoes. Cut in small cubes. Chop onion.

2. Melt butter in pan. Cook onion, leeks, garlic, stirring till soft not coloured for 5 minutes.

3. Add potatoes. Stir well. Put lid on pan. Cook gently further 4 minutes.

4. Tip in half watercress. Stir to wilt it. Add stock or water, salt, black pepper.

5. Boil. Reduce heat to simmer for 15 minutes. Tip in rest of watercress. Cook 5 minutes (check spuds are soft).

6. Remove from heat. Stir in mustard, cheese, lemon juice. Cool for a little. Blitz in liquidizer or processor. Taste. Add crème fraîche if using and little extra liquid if too thick. Adjust seasoning. Eat as is or top with croutons baked in olive oil, Parmesan, crumbled crispy bacon.

For 4

225 g/8 oz watercress
1 medium potato
1 leek
1 medium onion
2 cloves garlic, crushed
40 g/1½ oz butter
900 ml/1½ pints
  chicken or veg stock
Salt and pepper
50 g/2 oz Parmesan or
  Cheddar, grated, or
  crumbled Stilton
1 tbsp lemon juice
2 tsps made English
  mustard
3 tbsps crème fraîche
  (optional)
Extra Parmesan to serve

Sexy veggie

Who needs meat when you've got these around? I don't.

For 6
Little butter for greasing
2 tbsps freshly grated
   Parmesan
50 g/2 oz fresh white
   breadcrumbs
175 g/6 oz finely grated
   Gruyère or mature
   Cheddar cheese (or a
   mix)
4 large eggs, separated
150 ml/¼ pint single
   cream
Salt and black pepper
3 pinches cayenne
   pepper
2 tbsps warm water

Filling
Garlic mayo for spreading
   – or plain, curried, lime,
   herb (page 123)
Rocket and watercress
   or iceberg lettuce,
   chopped
Cherry tomatoes, halved
Cucumber, peeled and
   chopped small
Chopped fresh herbs
   (optional)
Drizzle balsamic
   (optional)

Cheese & leaf roller

Cheese roulade's a class machine. The lush cheese roller drives your crunchy salad.

Method

1. Butter a 35 x 27 cm/14 x 10½ in Swiss roll tin. Line with baking paper slightly larger than tin. Press into corners to make little rim. Sprinkle half the Parmesan evenly over it.

2. Preheat oven to 200°C/400°F/gas 6.

3. Mix breadcrumbs, Gruyère/Cheddar cheese, egg yolks, cream, seasoning and cayenne. Stir in water.

4. Whisk egg whites till stiff. Fold into cheese mix with metal spoon using light scooping movements to retain air.

5. Spread lightly and evenly over tin. Bake 10–15 minutes till risen and springy. Remove to rack.

6. Prep salad ingredients.

7. Sprinkle remaining Parmesan over another piece of baking paper the size of your tin. Turn roulade over onto cheese.

8. Peel paper off. Spread light layer of mayo and salad, drizzle balsamic.

9. Use paper to help roll roulade from one end to make a clumsy roll – it may crack and spill, but no problem.

10. Lift onto plate. Get some leaves on there. Slice and serve with warm bread and more salad.

⏱ TIME TRICK

Egg-wise, don't waste time with whites that won't whisk up. Use totally grease-free hands and utensils. And avoid any yolk getting in with the whites. Crack one at a time – yolk in one bowl, white in another – before adding to the main recipe.

Cheeky tarts

Creamy mushroom tart?
Or sparky tomato?
Make both.

Method

1. Preheat oven to 220°C/425°F/gas 7.

2. Slap butter in pan. Chuck mushrooms and garlic in. Fry gently with more butter if needed. Add wine. Bubble to evaporate.

3. Add herbs, soy, cream and seasoning. Remove from heat.

4. On a floured board roll half pastry into a rectangle 23 x 15 cm/9 x 6 in. Repeat with second bit.

5. Lay pastry bases on two lightly greased baking trays. With a sharp knife and without cutting through, run a line down the long sides only, about 2½ cm/1 in from the edges to puff up during cooking. Don't cut a line at the short sides. Prick the inner part of each tart with a fork.

6. Lay the mushroom mix inside one tart.

7. Spread the inside of the other with a layer of tapenade or tomato purée. Cover with cherry tomatoes rolled in oil, olives, basil, blobs of goats' cheese, bits of onion. Bake for 15 minutes.

For 4–6

375 g/13 oz pack butter puff pastry, defrosted

Mushroom bit

225 g/8 oz button or chestnut mushrooms, roughly chopped

2 cloves garlic, crushed

1 tbsp butter

1 tbsp white wine

Few leaves rosemary or tarragon, chopped

Few drops soy sauce

1 tbsp cream

Salt and black pepper

Tomato bit

350 g/12 oz cherry tomatoes

Olive oil

1 tbsp tapenade (page 123) or sun-dried tomato purée

Few black olives

Bit of goats' cheese

Slices of red onion

Basil leaves

Bubbling baked eggplant

Save time if you've got a stash of tomato sauce in your freezer or fridge. Or make from fresh – you've got ages.

Method

1. Preheat oven to 220°C/425°F/gas 7.

2. Drizzle olive oil over large baking tray.

3. Slice aubergines in 5 mm/¼ in circles.

4. Drizzle with bit more oil. Scatter basil over.

5. Bake for 10 minutes (or you can griddle them – page 60).

6. Prep tomato sauce and heat.

7. Grease a shallow baking or gratin dish with tiny bit of oil. Cover with thin layer of tomato sauce, sprinkle little cheese, layer of aubergines, seasoning, cheese.

8. Repeat till used up. Finish with layer of cheese, use more cheese if needed to cover aubergines.

9. Bake for 10 minutes or till hot and top bubbling.

For 4

2 large aubergines

1 x quantity tomato sauce (page 66) or 1 jar passata

Fresh basil leaves, torn

225 g/8 oz grated Parmesan or Cheddar

Eat with: Garlic bread and salad

Time cheat pizzas

Pizza cheats charter. 1. Make dough.
2. Griddle a bit immediately for thin
crisp pizza. 3. Leave the rest to rise.
4. Shape and slap in the freezer.
5. Top and bake whenever for
speedy deep lush pizza.

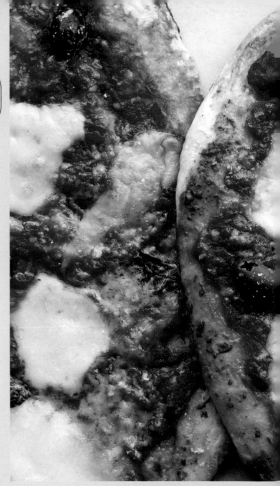

For 2–4 pizza bases
450 g/1 lb strong white
   bread flour
1 tsp salt
1 tsp caster sugar
2 x 7 g sachet fast action
   dried yeast
300 ml/½ pint warm
   water
2 tbsps good olive oil

TIME
TRICK
**Prep topping
ingredients before you
get the frozen bases
out. Frozen bases
make easier topping.**

Basic pizza dough for rolling & stashing

A tasty olive oil dough makes all
the difference. Use instantly for
thin crispy pizzas or freeze and
fast top for any time you like.
Note: sort out loads for parties.

Method
1. Sift flour and salt into bowl. Add sugar and yeast.
2. Pour in water and olive oil. Mix together with your
fingers.
3. Work dough into a soft warm ball. Add a drop more
water if needed.
4. Kneading by hand? Slap onto floured board. Punch,
pull, thump and knead for 10 minutes till soft and elastic.
5. Using mixer? Slap into machine. Mix with dough hook
for 8 minutes.
6. Put dough in large bowl. Pop carrier or large plastic
bag on top. Leave in warm place for 1 hour or till doubled.
7. Meantime, lightly oil four large baking trays.
8. Divide dough into 2 or 4. Roll each section out into
circles or rectangles. Leave covered on baking trays to
rise again for 15–20 minutes.
9. Cook one or more pizzas if you want (see opposite).
Slide the rest into freezer on trays. Take off trays when
hard (about 2 hours). Store in large freezer bags.

The thin crispy griddled one

Like pizza cooked in woodfire ovens; charred and smoky. Crispy, speedy and impressive. Note: fast. No need for dough rising.

Method

1. Make basic dough (up to and including STEP 5).
2. Break off a small piece. (Put rest to rise for bases.)
3. Roll out on floured board till just smaller than your griddle.
4. Brush griddle with bit of olive oil. Put on very high heat.
5. Slap dough down. It will bubble and maybe puff. Cook 1 minute or till done. Turn. Cook another minute.
6. Put grill on to max heat.
7. Mix garlic into tomato sauce. Spread very thinly on base. Chuck on olives, herbs, Parmesan, seasoning, drizzle with little olive oil.
8. Grill for 1–2 minutes or till slightly charred, crisp and sizzling.

The deep lush baked one

Top'n'bake your frozen bases with these tomato combos. Maybe add prosciutto, Parma ham, pepperoni, anchovies, mix of cheeses, whatever. Your choice, your pizza.

Cool tomato pizza – no cheese
Method

1. Preheat oven to 230°C/400°F/gas 6.
2. Stick tomatoes in a bowl with 2 tablespoons olive oil, oregano, pinch of sugar.
3. Spread on bases. Sprinkle garlic, basil, drizzle olive oil. Sit pizzas on oiled tray. Bake 15–20 minutes.

Margherita
Method

1. Preheat oven to 230°C/400°F/gas 6.
2. Mix garlic into sauce. Spread on bases.
3. Scatter olives, mozzarella, Parmesan, basil.
4. Drizzle with olive oil. Bake 15–20 minutes.

The thin crispy one

1 x first-stage pizza dough
Bit of tomato sauce (page 66) or sugocasa or passata
1 clove garlic, crushed
Few black olives
Few basil leaves or pinch of oregano
Freshly grated Parmesan
Salt and black pepper
Olive oil

VARIATIONS

THE MEATY ONE
Add a bit of ham, salami or pepperoni but keep it thin.
THE GARLIC ONE
Mix olive oil with 2 cloves crushed garlic, herbs, seasoning, bit of chopped tomato.

Cool tomato pizza

400 g/14 oz can chopped tomatoes or 225 g/8 oz fresh tomatoes, chopped
2–3 tbsps good olive oil
2 pinches dried oregano
3 cloves sliced garlic
Few basil leaves
Salt and black pepper

Margherita

1 quantity tomato sauce (page 66) or jar sugocasa or passata
2 cloves garlic, crushed
Few black olives
Slices of mozzarella
Few basil leaves
Freshly grated Parmesan
Olive oil to drizzle

30 minutes

Kebabs

I love these babes on sticks. Sizzle 'em on the barbie when it's hot. Stick 'em on the grill pan when it's not. Note: using wooden skewers? Soak in cold water for 20 minutes to stop them flaming.

For 4
4 chicken breasts, cut in chunks
Bay leaves (optional)

Barbecue sauce
1 tbsp sunflower oil
1 medium onion, chopped
1 clove garlic, chopped
Few gratings peeled ginger (or 3 pinches dried ginger)
2 tbsps Worcestershire sauce
3 tbsps tomato ketchup
1½ tbsps malt vinegar
1 tbsp orange juice
1½ tbsps soft brown sugar
Ginger wine or orange juice if needed

Sticky barbecue chicken skewers

Check out your chicken with this marvellous barbie sauce. Try it on pork too (chops, skewers, spare ribs, pork fillet). It's kind of addictive. (Lick your fingers.) Great with rice and salad.

Method

1. Heat oil in small pan. Add onion, garlic. Cook on low heat for 3 minutes without colouring. Add other sauce ingredients. Boil. Simmer for 3 minutes. Blitz with hand blender or in blender.
2. Put chicken into bowl with two-thirds sauce. Turn to coat. Leave 5 minutes.
3. Preheat grill to max. Thread chicken on 4 metal or presoaked wooden skewers. Alternate with bay leaves if using.
4. Lay skewers on rack over grill pan. Turn frequently for 10 minutes or till chicken is white all through but still moist and tender. Test with knife.
5. Meantime, stick last third of sauce to heat in pan with bit of juice or ginger wine to thin. Drizzle over kebabs when ready to serve.

VARIATION
TANDOORI CHICKEN
At STEP 1 mix chicken with juice of 1 lemon and little salt. At STEP 2 blitz up 240 ml/8 fl oz natural yogurt, 1 clove garlic, 1 chopped shallot, 2.5 cm/1 in piece ginger, 1 small de-seeded red chilli, 2 tsps tomato purée, 2 tsps garam masala, pinch of paprika. Pour over chicken. Leave, then cook as main recipe.

Halloumi vegetable skewers

Hmmm ... one of life's big questions. Which of the many cool veg should this cheese sit next to?

Method

1. Throw cheese and veg into big bowl.

2. Pour oil, garlic, lemon and herbs over. Stir to coat. Leave 10 minutes.

3. Line grill pan with foil. Preheat grill to high.

4. Stick cheese, veg and bay leaves, if using, onto metal or presoaked wooden skewers

5. Grill on rack. Turn every few minutes for 8–10 minutes, brushing with marinade if dry, till cheese is hot and soft, veg softening but a bit crisp still.

6. Drizzle with remaining marinade, salsa verde (page 55), dip in lime or harissa or garlic mayo (page 123).

For 4

450 g/1 lb halloumi cheese, cubed
3 courgettes, chunked
2 red peppers, de-seeded and chunked
4 firm tomatoes, halved or quartered
Few button mushrooms, de-stalked
2 red onions, quartered
Bay leaves (optional)

Marinade

5 tbsps good olive oil
2 fat cloves garlic, crushed
Juice of 1 lemon
2 pinches of dried or handful fresh chopped parsley or basil
Sea salt and black pepper

Eat with: Couscous salad (page 69) and warm flatbread.

Lamb kebabs

A damned fine kebab.

Method

1. Slap meat into a large bowl.

2. Combine rest of ingredients. Tip over meat. Mix. Leave to marinate.

3. Preheat grill to max. Slip meat onto metal skewers. Alternate with bay leaves, if using.

4. Lay on rack over grill pan. Grill for few minutes each side till meat is crunchy outside, pink and tender inside.

For 4–6

900 g/2 lb cubed lamb steak, leg or fillet
1½ tbsps sweet paprika
1 tbsp olive oil
Juice of a lemon
1 clove garlic, crushed
2 tbsps oregano or thyme
Sea salt and black pepper
Bay leaves (optional)

WHY NOT?

Team it up with natural yogurt and jam it in a pitta pocket with a champion salad?

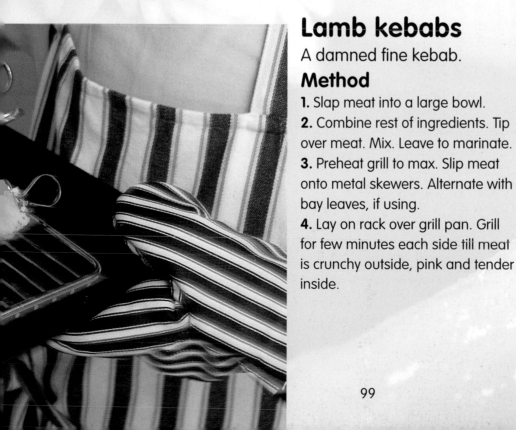

Tex-Mex

What's firey, limey? Coriander. Sour cream. Salsas.
Guacamole. Loadsa chilli. Peppers. Spices. Meat. Cheese.
Veggie. Own tortillas. Stack 'em. Wrap 'em. Get on texting.
MSNing. Download Tex-Mex. Music on. Go party.

Makes 10–12
225 g/8 oz plain white
 flour
1 tsp salt
25 g/1 oz white
 vegetable fat or lard
125 ml/4 fl oz warm
 water

Own tortillas

A quick bit of rubbing in then rolling out. A thin soft tortilla cooks
in less than a minute plus tastes and wraps soooo much better
than a bought one.

Method

1. Sift flour and salt into large bowl.
2. Drop fat into flour. Using your fingertips, rub the fat quickly and lightly
into the flour with a rubbing motion till it disappears.
3. Add water bit by bit, mixing in with a fork. Draw dough together into a
ball with your fingers. Knead to make it smooth.
4. Cover bowl with cloth. Leave at least 10–15 mins.

To make

1. Cover a board or flat surface with a light layer
of flour.
2. Divide dough into 10 small balls.
3. Flour a rolling pin. Sit first ball on board. Flatten
slightly to establish circular shape. Roll out very
lightly (15–20 cm/6–8 in diameter). It may stick a
bit. Don't panic. Just re-roll on re-floured surface.
(Some people roll it between clingfilm.) If very
uneven cut to perfect shape – or leave it.
4. Repeat till dough used up. Heat ungreased
crêpe or flatish frying pan.
5. Slap tortilla down when really hot. Cook till just
done – 1–2 minutes per side. You want them
pliable, still soft with light brown patches.
6. Cover with tea towel immediately or tortillas
dry out. Fill when ready. Freeze extras.

Tostadas

Fried tortillas transform into plate-sized tortilla crisps for stacking. Pile them high or let people DIY at the table. Note: cooked tortillas make a thicker crisp than uncooked.

Method

1. Heat oil in frying pan. Fry each tortilla till crisp each side.

2. Keep warm and take all to table with bowls of extras, or stack.

3. Spread layer mashed beans, shredded lettuce (optional sparky dressing), sliced chicken, guacamole, cheese.

Ingredients
Olive or sunflower oil
1–2 cooked or uncooked tortillas per person

Toppings, choose from:
Smashed bean mix (page 123)
1 iceberg lettuce, shredded
Salad dressing (optional) (page 122)
2 cooked chicken breasts or chicken from cold roast, shredded
Guacamole (page 38) or sliced avocados
Grated Cheddar cheese or crumbled feta

30 minutes

For 4

2 large skinless chicken
   breasts
2 limes, juiced
1 tbsp caster sugar
1 tsp dried oregano
Pinch cinnamon
Pinch cayenne pepper
8 home-made (page
   100) or bought tortillas

Stir-fry

2 tbsps sunflower oil
1 red onion, thinly sliced
1 small red chilli,
   de-seeded and finely
   sliced
1 red pepper, cut in strips
   and de-seeded
1 orange pepper, cut in
   strips and de-seeded

Extras

Salsa
Cheddar
Guacamole
Sour cream

VARIATION
BEEF FAJITAS
Sub 350 g/10 oz
rump steak for
chicken.

Chicken fajitas

Be neat. Wrap these up for people so they can get back to chatting and dancing. For more intimate gatherings lay things out on your table. This is ultimate cool. Lime tenderized chicken stir-fried with onions and peppers. Works with tofu, mushrooms or quorn for veggies.

Method

1. Slice chicken into 1 cm/½ in strips. Chuck into bowl with lime juice, sugar, dried oregano, spices. Leave.

2. Meantime make tortilla dough. Prep stir-fry veg and extras while dough is resting. (Using ready-made? Prep them ready for warming.)

3. Cook tortillas on griddle (see page 100). Keep warm in tea towel.

4. Heat oil in large frying pan or wok. Stir-fry drained chicken for 5 minutes.

5. Add onions, peppers, chilli. Stir-fry 3–4 minutes till chicken cooked white throughout and veg soft.

6. Divide mix between tortillas with bit of salsa, Cheddar, guacamole (page 38), sour cream. Wrap. Eat.

Quesadillas

A wicked treat – sometimes! Team them up with the usual suspects.

Method

1. Lay tortillas out. Slap spoonful of beans topped with both cheeses, chilli or jalapeños, coriander and squeeze of lime on one quarter portion of each one.

2. Fold tortilla in half then in half again to make a triangular parcel.

3. Dampen inner edges and press down to seal. Pin with 2 or 3 cocktail sticks if tricky. (Always take them out before serving to avoid choking.)

4. Pour oil into frying pan. It should reach a third of the way up parcels. Fry quesadillas in batches till cooked through, golden. Drain on kitchen paper. Eat with sour cream, salsa, guacamole (page 38).

For 4

1 batch tortillas (see page 100)
1 can refried beans
225 g/8 oz Cheddar, grated
110 g/4 oz mozzarella, chopped small
2 chillies, de-seeded and finely chopped or few pickled jalapeños
1 tbsp coriander, finely chopped
1 lime
Sunflower or vegetable oil for frying

VARIATION

FAST NO-FRY OPTION Lay freshly cooked or bought tortillas on hot griddle. Sprinkle shredded mozzarella or grated Cheddar over one half. Fold over and press edges down. Cook for 1 minute. Turn and cook 1 minute. Cut into three wedges. Eat immediately. Some like it hot: slap fresh chopped and de-seeded chilli in there.

Risotto ... relaxing

Risotto's the real deal and these two stand out from the crowd. They push at the time-barrier but they're worth it. Use risotto rice (arborio's cool, vialone nano's creamier). And great stock. Your own's best (page 122) or buy in some quality.

For 4

1 litre/1¾ pints chicken or vegetable stock
10 g/½ oz dried mushrooms
50 g/2 oz butter
1 medium onion, finely chopped
2 cloves garlic, crushed
175 g/6 oz chestnut mushrooms, chopped
350 g/12 oz arborio or vialone nano rice
150 ml/5 fl oz white wine (or more stock)
1 lemon
1 tsp soy sauce
Salt and pepper
1 tbsp crème fraîche
50 g/2 oz freshly grated Parmesan, plus extra for sprinkling

WHY NOT?

Make up a rice bowl meal. Rinse 150 g/ 5 oz basmati rice in sieve. Chuck in pan with 300 ml/10 fl oz cold water. Boil. Cover. Simmer gently for 10 minutes or till water absorbed. Turn off heat. Leave to stand for 5 minutes. Drain. Fluff with fork. Top with griddled chicken, fish, beef, pan-fried tofu, stir-fried pak choi.

Mushroom risotto

Brilliant. Looks like mushroom porridge but you've got waves of different flavours in there. Keep the bits of mushroom chunky. The dried jobs give your palate a different sort of hit, then there's back-up from some other great flavours. Note: good if you feel hyper. Rice sorts you out and the stirring's therapeutic.

Method

1. Put bought or own stock into pan. Bring to high heat then keep it warm.

2. Put dried mushrooms to soak in bowl with 2–3 tablespoons hot stock.

3. Slap butter to melt in largish pan. Fling onion in to fry gently 1–2 minutes. Tip fresh mushrooms in with garlic to fry 1–2 minutes.

4. Add rice, stirring to coat grains. Tip in wine. Let it bubble while you stir till it's about soaked in. Add dried mushrooms and liquid.

5. Pour a ladle of hot stock in with rice. Stir till nearly absorbed. Add another. Continue this bit by bit over 10–15 minutes till all stock is used and rice is going soft and creamy. Taste it. Add bit more wine or stock if it needs. You want it a bit soupy. Squeeze in juice of half lemon. Taste and add more if you like.

6. Remove from heat. Add soy, salt and pepper. Mix in crème fraîche, Parmesan. Serve in bowls or on plates. Top with extra Parmesan.

Salmon, cheese & green leaf risotto

Is this the ultimate risotto? In our house, yes. Best made with hot-smoked salmon (not the ordinary oily one). Get this at the deli or good supermarket in vacuum packs. Use bits of cooked salmon fillet if they don't have it. Note: don't rush your risotto.

Method

1. Pour own or bought stock into a pan and get it hot. Keep it warm.

2. Slap butter to melt in another pan. Cook onion and garlic gently on a low heat for a few minutes till soft, not coloured.

3. Turn up the heat a bit. Tip rice into the pan. Stir to coat. Tip wine in. It will splutter and crackle. Don't worry. Cook, stirring till it's absorbed.

4. Add a ladle of hot stock, stirring as you go. When nearly absorbed add another, continuing over 10–15 minutes till all used. Bite into rice to check it is soft. Sometimes it needs a bit more liquid. It wants to be a bit soupy.

5. Turn off heat. Stir in cheese, crème fraîche, spinach or rocket, bits of salmon, few herbs, season. Add lemon juice. Taste and adjust. Top with few herbs and grated Cheddar. Serve in soup bowls.

VARIATIONS

PEA AND ASPARAGUS
At STEP 4 add frozen peas when half stock in. At STEP 5 sub cooked asparagus tips for smoked salmon.
CHICKEN, HAM AND CHEESE
At STEP 5 add small chunks of gammon, shredded cooked chicken and Cheddar instead of smoked salmon. Note: make sure chicken is thoroughly heated before serving.

For 4

- 1.2 litres/2 pints chicken, fish or vegetable stock
- 75 g/3 oz butter
- 1 medium to large onion, very finely chopped
- 2 cloves garlic, crushed
- 225 g/8 oz arborio or vialone nano rice
- 150 ml/5 fl oz white wine
- 50 g/2 oz very mature Cheddar cheese, grated
- 225 g/8 oz hot-smoked salmon, broken in bits
- 50 g/2 oz young spinach leaves or rocket
- 2 tsps fresh dill, parsley, or coriander, finely chopped
- 50 ml/2 fl oz crème fraîche or single cream
- Salt and black pepper
- Squeeze lemon juice
- Extra Cheddar or Parmesan for sprinkling

Family favourites

Everyone cooks in our house, which means cooking together. OK it can get a bit bitter when we're all in the kitchen, but we have a great laugh and the eating's always real. Have a go at these – our family favourites. But always remember who's in charge of the kitchen. In your case, it's you. In mine, I am.

For 4
1–2 tbsps Dijon mustard
1 tsp white wine vinegar
Sea salt and pepper
4 chicken breasts

Filling options
Garlic butter
50 g/2 oz soft butter
2 plump cloves of garlic,
  crushed and finely
  chopped
Herb of choice

Ham & cheese
2 slices thin ham
Thin sliced or grated
  Cheddar, fontina or
  Gruyère

Coating
50 g/2 oz crustless stale
  white bread
50 g/2 oz Parmesan,
  finely grated
10 g/½ oz soft butter

Eat with: Speedy fried
spuds and sparky salad

Chicken kievs

So who wants what in their chicken kiev? Dad likes his unfilled. I stuff them with garlic butter for Mum and me. It's cheese and ham filling for my mates, Joe and Tom. That's the one dish. Everyone sorted.

Method

1. Preheat oven to 230°C/450°F/gas 8.
2. Mix mustard, vinegar, salt and pepper in a large shallow dish for marinade.
3. Put any chicken you won't be filling into dish and coat it.
4. Prep fillings for rest of chicken. Slice ham and cheese. Cream butter, garlic and herbs in a bowl.
5. Sit chicken on a flat board. Slash laterally across the centre of each, two-thirds through. Tuck filling into the slash. Avoid the edges to avoid oozing. Press down firmly to seal the edges.
6. Add all chicken to marinade dish. Turn and leave it.
7. Meantime blitz bread in processor with butter and Parmesan.
8. Tip onto a large plate. Add all chicken bits, turning to coat. Sit chicken on a baking tray. Cook for 15–20 minutes. Test for doneness by poking with a sharp knife. Meat should be white through and moist. Delicious.

Salmon fishcakes

The real thing. See 'em live at a plate near you. Top dog fishcakes.
Top tip: use yesterday's mash to speed things up, but work fast from scratch for a gourmet fishcake.

Makes 6

175 g/6 oz old potatoes, peeled and cut in chunks
50 g/2 oz butter
1 shallot or small onion, finely chopped
1 clove garlic, crushed
350 g/12 oz skinless, boneless salmon fillet
125 ml/4 fl oz white wine or apple juice
75 g/3 oz crustless bread
Lemon or lime juice
1 tsp English mustard
1 tbsp fresh dill, coriander or parsley
Sea salt and black pepper
Little plain flour for dusting
1 beaten egg for coating
Olive oil
Crème fraîche (optional)

Eat with: Posh mushy peas. Great with a piece of crisp streaky bacon on top. Dip in sweet chilli sauce, ketchup or garlic mayo.

WHY NOT?
Team with spinach. Wash leaves. Don't drain. Slap in pan (no water, lid on). Cook 2–3 minutes. Drain well. Toss in a little butter and finely chopped garlic.

Method

1. Slide spuds into a small pan of boiling salted water. Cook fast till soft.

2. Meantime melt half the butter in another pan. Gently fry shallot and garlic for 2 minutes till soft, not coloured.

3. Add the salmon (in 3 cm cubes), wine or juice and seasoning. Cover. Cook till done or 4 minutes.

4. Meantime blitz the bread. Spread fine crumbs on a large plate.

5. Drain cooked fish mix in a sieve over a bowl. Save the liquid. Spread fish mix over a large plate. Flake it up with a fork.

6. Drain spuds well. Tip them back in the pan. Shake over heat to dry for a few seconds. Then bash with masher or fork, adding lemon or lime juice and mustard.

7. Tip mash, fish, chopped herbs, seasoning into a large bowl, mixing gently with a fork. Shape the mix into small cakes or fingers.

8. Assemble coating: spread flour over a plate or board. Beat egg in a shallow dish. Get breadcrumbs. Dip and turn fishcakes in flour first, egg (let excess drip off), then roll in breadcrumbs.

9. Heat oil and remaining butter in a frying pan. Fry cakes for 3 minutes per side or till hot all through and golden.

10. Meantime, heat reserved fish liquid with bit of crème fraîche plus extra wine or juice if you need. Awesome drizzled round fishcakes.

30 minutes

For 4

2 tbsps sunflower oil
1 medium onion,
    chopped small
2 cloves garlic, crushed
8 chestnut mushrooms,
    sliced
300 ml/10 fl oz cider or
    apple juice
1 x 410 g/14 oz tin baked
    beans
1 x 410 g/14 oz tin haricot
    or butter beans, drained
1 tsp made mustard
Few shakes
    Worcestershire sauce
1 tsp tomato purée
2–3 tbsps fresh
    coriander, parsley or
    thyme, chopped
Black pepper
1 tbsp crème fraîche
Drizzle of sherry
225–275 g/8–10 oz
    chorizo sausage, sliced
3–4 oz crustless bread

WHY NOT?
Sub chorizo with
bits of best pork
sausage.

VEGGIE OPTION
When Poll and Katie
are back (veggie
and vegan), I spoon
off a couple of
portions of bean
mix before the
chorizo goes in,
sub in veggie
sausage or a load
more garlic
mushrooms.

Cracking cassoulet

Cheat's classic. Cassoulet takes hours to cook, which is great if you have time, but a pain in the butt if not. So sort this fast then go catch a movie. Or collapse for a family night on the sofa. Note: good with dollops of apple chutney (page 124).

Method

1. Heat oil in saucepan or small casserole dish. Slap onion in. Cook gently without colouring for 3–4 minutes.

2. Add garlic and mushrooms. Stir to coat. Cook very gently for another few minutes.

3. Tip in cider or juice. Let it bubble for 2 minutes.

4. Tip in tins of beans. Mix. Add drizzle of sherry, mustard, Worcestershire sauce, purée, a third of the chopped herb and loads of ground pepper.

5. Let it simmer very gently, checking it never threatens to dry out.

6. Brush frying pan with thinnest layer of oil. Gently fry the chorizo slices on each side till coloured but still quite soft. Drain. Tip into beans and mix. Let the mixture simmer very gently.

7. Preheat grill. Blitz bread and rest of herbs in processor.

8. Spoon bean mix into individual ovenproof dishes or one large shallow one. Sprinkle breadcrumbs on top.

9. Sit dishes on rack in grill pan. Cook for 3–4 minutes till just brown.

Easy cheese soufflés

Light. High. These stretch the time boundaries but look and taste awesome. Get your digi camera out. Get 'em in the family album.

Method

1. Preheat oven to 200°C/400°F/gas 6. Put baking tray on shelf with room above it.

2. Prep 8 x 7½ cm or 2¾ inch ramekins. Grease lightly with extra butter. Divide coating Parmesan between dishes (helps rising). Roll each one fast so it sticks to base and sides. Needn't be perfect.

3. Melt butter in pan. Add sifted flour, mustard, cayenne or nutmeg. Let it bubble as you stir for 1 minute. Take pan off heat. Pour milk in gradually, beating with wooden spoon or balloon whisk.

4. When sauce is smooth, slap back onto heat and bring to boil. Let mix bubble for 2 minutes. Keep whisking so it doesn't burn. It gets thick. Don't panic. The process stops the soufflé tasting floury.

5. Take sauce off heat. Add cheese, egg yolks, salt, pepper, a few drops of lemon juice. Beat really well.

6. Whisk egg whites with a grease-free electric or hand whisk till stiff. Stir one tablespoonful into the sauce. Tip the rest in then fold into the sauce using large, scoopy, light movements to retain the air.

7. Fill ramekins to just over two-thirds full. For top-hat effect, run your finger in a circle round the mix.

8. Sit soufflés on baking tray. Bake 11–12 minutes before opening door. Done means high, wobbly. A skewer poked in comes out nearly clean. Give extra time if needed. Eat immediately.

For 4

Bit of soft, melted butter for greasing
10 g/½ oz finely grated Parmesan for coating
35 g/1½ oz butter
25 g/1 oz plain white flour
½ tsp dry mustard
Pinch cayenne pepper or nutmeg
300 ml/½ pint milk
Few drops lemon juice
75 g/3 oz mature Cheddar, Gruyère or Parmesan, finely grated
4 large eggs, separated
Salt and black pepper

Eat with: Grated Parmesan, salsa verde for dipping (page 55) and sparky salad.

VARIATION

CHEESE AND COURGETTE
At STEP 2 dice 175 g/ 6 oz courgettes. Fry in a little butter till just soft. At STEP 5 add to sauce. At STEP 7 make sure each ramekin gets some.

For 4

2 x lean racks of lamb,
  each with 6 small
  cutlets, fat trimmed
1–2 tbsps Dijon mustard
50 g/2 oz soft butter
2 cloves garlic
110 g/4 oz white
  crustless bread
  (stale is best)
2 tbsps finely chopped
  fresh herbs: parsley,
  tarragon, mint, thyme,
  chives or a mix
Salt and black pepper
3 heaped tbsps
  redcurrant jelly
300 ml/10 fl oz wine or
  water

TIME TRICK

Skip herb crust. Buy
lamb with fat. Salt and
score with sharp knife.
Or roll in chopped
herbs. Roast as basic.

Lamb in a rack with herb crust

A turbo-charged roast with an ultra cool crust. Who gets to
carve? You do. Note: cooking meat on the bone always makes
for a sweet eat.

Method

1. Preheat oven to 220°C/425°F/gas 7.

2. Trim any excess fat off top of rack with sharp knife (needn't be neat).

3. Make herb crust. Blitz bread, garlic and herbs. Chuck in a bowl with salt,
butter, mustard, seasoning. Mix to soft paste.

4. Spread paste evenly over racks, pressing to keep in place.

5. Slap meat into a roasting tin, crust side up. Roast for 15 minutes.

6. When lamb's done (still a bit pink inside – check with knife), rest it
somewhere warm.

7. Melt redcurrant jelly with wine or water in roasting tin.

8. Cut rack between bones to separate chops. Tip any juices in with
redcurrant gravy. Drizzle over lamb. Delicious with new potatoes, minty
peas and a sharp, suited salad.

Roast sweet'n'salty duck with jammy sauce and garlic mash

A load of random ingredients. Bit of duck. Jam. Few spuds. Bit of red wine. Few spices, garlic. Tom brought this recipe back home with a load of washing. Tastes awesome. Uni life, eh!

Method

1. Preheat oven to 220°C/425°F/gas 7.

2. Tip sugar, salt and spice onto a large plate. Mix well.

3. Slash fat on each duck 4 or 5 times diagonally across.

4. Lay this side down in spice mix. Press down. Sit plate on top with all kitchen weights to help marinate.

5. Start mash. Slap peeled, chunked spuds to boil with garlic. Boil 15 minutes or till soft.

6. Start duck. Slap it fat side down on hot griddle pan for 2 minutes or till browned. Turn. Sizzle 2 minutes. Sit duck on a rack in a roasting tin. Roast 10–15 minutes.

7. Sort sauce. Spoon jam into a small pan with wine (or port or stock). Get it bubbling. Stir to reduce over a gentle heat for 5 minutes.

8. Check duck with a sharp knife (a bit pink inside). Relax it in warm place (save duck fat for cooking).

9. Drain spuds and garlic. Prep mash as page 84 adding butter, hot milk, mustard and spring onion.

10. Working fast, sit duck on flat board. Carve diagonally across. Tip juices into warmed jammy sauce. Lay duck on piled mash, drizzle with sauce. Throw on salad and dressing.

For 4
4 duck breasts
2 tsps sugar
1 tsp salt
1 tsp five spice mix

Mash
900 g/2 lb old potatoes
2 cloves garlic
50 g/2 oz butter
125 ml/4 fl oz milk
2 spring onions, sliced
Salt and black pepper

Jammy sauce
2–3 tbsps Morello cherry jam (with cherry bits)
175 g/6 fl oz red wine, port, chicken or veg stock (page 122)

Eat with: Salad and dressing

30 minutes

Stuffed crêpes

Don't hold back. These roll, fold, fill, flap. Got mates round? Happy-Stuff-Your-Own-Crêpes-Day.

For 8–10 crêpes

Crêpe batter
175 g/6 oz plain white flour
Good pinch salt
Freshly ground black pepper
2 large eggs
1 extra egg yolk
425 ml/¾ pint milk
2 tsps butter, melted
2 tsps poppy seeds or finely chopped fresh dill or chives

Crêpe fillings

Ham & cheese
Bit of mango chutney, thin ham, grated Cheddar.

Honey garlic prawns
Fry 2 chopped spring onions, 1 clove crushed garlic, little grated ginger in oil for 3 minutes. Add handful cooked prawns. Turn to heat through. Drizzle a little runny honey, squeeze of lime, pepper, splash of soy.

Spinach & cheese
Cook young spinach for 3 minutes in pan with 1 tablespoon water. Drain. Mix with crushed garlic, pepper, low fat crème fraîche and Cheddar.

Cheese & tuna
As above. Skip spinach. sub tuna and spring onion.

Crispy baked filled crêpes

These are light and lacy. Stick poppy seeds or herbs in the batter if you want. Fill with ham and cheese, honey garlic prawns, spinach and cheese or our best mate: spring onion, cheese and tuna.

Method

For batter

1. Blitz first six ingredients in processor, or sift flour and salt into large bowl with pepper. Make dent in centre. Chuck eggs and yolk in with bit of milk. Beat continuously with balloon whisk, slowly pouring rest of milk to make a smooth batter.

2. Stir in seeds, herbs, melted butter. Batter can be made hours ahead. Store in fridge. Mix before frying.

To cook

1. Heat a crêpe or flat pan. Brush with a little butter. Heat till sizzling.

2. When hot (not burned), pour batter from jug or spoon into pan.

3. Swirl the batter round to coat base with a thin layer. Bubble for 1 minute

or till crisp. Loosen round sides with spatula. Slide under crêpe to lift and turn. Cook 1 minute or till crisp.

4. Fill or stack between greaseproof till needed.

To fill

1. Preheat oven to 220°C/425°F/gas 7.

2. Lay cooked crêpes out flat. Pile any of the fillings onto one quarter.

3. Fold crêpe in half then again to make triangular wedge.

4. Sit single or multiple crêpes on baking tray. Bake 10 minutes.

Chicken, ham, cheese & tomato

Roll your own. Slap some cold chicken, ham or gammon and other bonus features in there. Got some Bolognese sauce left over?

Method

1. Preheat oven to 220°C/425°F/ gas 7.

2. Lay crêpes flat. Smear a bit of tomato sauce or passata with added garlic over them.

3. Place meats and grated cheese down the centre.

4. Roll. Put in lightly greased medium-sized shallow dish.

5. Spoon tomato sauce or passata round crêpes. Sprinkle more cheese.

6. Bake 10–15 minutes till hot through and sizzling.

Ingredients
Cold roast chicken, torn
Bits of cold gammon, sliced and diced, or good bought ham
Gruyère, Cheddar or Parmesan, grated
Home-made tomato sauce (page 66) or jar passata (crushed tomato) with crushed garlic added

Mushroom crêpe roll

Veggies often get a rough deal of it. Not with this one.

Dedicated to my sister, Polly.

Method

1. Preheat oven to 220°C/425°F/gas 7.

2. Melt a bit of butter in a pan. Add garlic and mushrooms. Saute for a few minutes till soft.

3. Season with salt, loads of pepper. Stir in tarragon and crème fraîche.

4. Place filling down side of crêpe.

5. Roll. Put in small shallow lightly greased dish.

6. Grate a bit of cheese over. Bake 10 mins or till lovely and sizzling.

For 1
Little butter
1 clove garlic, crushed
4 or 5 button or chestnut mushrooms, chopped
Salt and black pepper
Few fresh tarragon leaves, chopped
1 tbsp low fat crème fraîche
1 crêpe
Gruyère, Cheddar or Parmesan, grated

Curry night – home-style

Everyone I know loves a curry. These are curries in a hurry. Good for family nights or when you have mates round.

For 4
75 g/3 oz butter
1 medium onion, finely
  diced
4 cloves garlic, crushed
Pinch salt
½ tsp cayenne pepper
½ tsp chilli powder
3 tsps sweet paprika
2 tsps garam masala
2 tsps ground coriander
1 cinnamon stick
4 cardamom pods,
  crushed
700 g/1¼ pint bottle
  passata (crushed
  tomatoes)
2 tbsps tomato purée
2 tbsps red wine vinegar
1 tbsp fresh grated
  ginger
4 skinless chicken
  breasts, diced
200 ml/7 fl oz double
  cream
150 ml/5 fl oz natural
  yogurt
Fresh coriander
Rice

Eat with: warmed naan
bread and salad.

Red butter chicken

A cool and creamy curry. Spoon it up with loads of poppadoms and mango chutney. Team it with other curries for a banquet.

Method

1. Slap butter to melt in large casserole or pan. Add onion, garlic, pinch of salt. Cook gently for 2 minutes. Add other spices. Cook till onion is soft.
2. Add passata, tomato purée, vinegar, ginger, and stir. Bring mix to boil. Simmer on reduced heat for 10 minutes.
3. Chuck chicken bits in pan. Stir to coat. Tip in cream and yogurt. Lower heat. Cook at gentle simmer for 10 minutes or till chicken is cooked white through.
4. Meantime cook rice. Stir coriander into chicken. Serve.

Potato, pea & mushroom curry

Great with a poppadom and a bit of rice. Partners creamy butter chicken. While you do that one, get a mate to do this one.

Method

1. Heat oil in a large pan. Slap in onion and pinch salt. Cook gently till soft for 2 minutes.

2. Add garlic, cumin and mustard seed. Cook and stir for 2 minutes.

3. Add turmeric, chilli, potatoes, tomatoes, mushrooms, little coriander. Cook over very low heat, 10 minutes. Stir so it doesn't burn.

4. Add peas plus little water if dry. Cook 3–4 minutes. Sprinkle with rest of coriander.

For 4

2 tbsps groundnut or sunflower oil

1 small onion, finely chopped

Salt

4 cloves garlic, crushed

½ tsp cumin seeds, crushed

½ tsp mustard seeds, crushed

½ tsp chilli powder

½ tsp turmeric

1 green chilli, de-seeded and finely chopped

3 tomatoes, roughly chopped

400 g/14 oz button mushrooms, washed, stalked and sliced

2 medium cold cooked potatoes, cubed

Cup of defrosted peas

Fresh coriander, chopped

Fast tikka masala dhal

My sisters make this all the time. It's vegan and veggie. Creamed coconut makes it a bit sexy.

1. Stick lentils in sieve under tap. Wash. Leave to drain.

2. Heat oil in large heavy-bottomed pan. Add onion plus pinch salt. Soften without colouring.

3. Add garlic and chilli. Stir in masala paste. Stir and cook gently for a minute or two. Throw washed lentils in. Stir round to coat.

4. Tip hot water into jug with creamed coconut. Stir. Add tomato purée, chutney.

5. Add to pan with juice of half a lemon and cinnamon stick. Stir, simmer for 15 minutes. Lentils swell. Stir and add bit more water if you need.

6. When cooked and creamy-thick, taste. Add more lemon if you like and loads of fresh coriander.

For 4

225 g/8 oz red lentils

2 tbsps groundnut or sunflower oil

1 large onion, chopped

Salt

4 cloves garlic, crushed

½–1 green chilli, de-seeded and finely chopped

2 tbsps tikka masala paste

1 lemon

1 cinnamon stick (optional)

110 g/4 oz creamed coconut

1 litre /1¾ pints hot water

1 tbsp mango chutney

2 tbsps tomato purée

Large bunch fresh coriander, chopped

30 minutes

Perfect puddings

What can I say? Enjoy yourself totally with these guys.

For 4
60 g/2½ oz soft butter
60 g/2½ oz good quality
   dark chocolate, broken
   into squares
½ tsp orange rind
2 tsps black coffee
2 medium eggs plus 2
   egg yolks
50 g/2 oz caster sugar
50 g/2 oz plain flour

Eat with: Fresh
raspberries, crème
fraîche, ice-cream,
whipped cream, custard

Shockingly good chocolate puds

Hot chocolate fudge puddings with an orange hit. Get your spoon into the oozy middle.

Method

1. Preheat oven to 180°C/350°F/gas 4. Slap in a baking tray. Lightly grease 4 x 150 ml ramekins.

2. Set bowl over pan of simmering water without base touching the water. Slap in butter, chocolate, orange rind, coffee. Let it melt gently. Mix it.

3. Meantime stick eggs and sugar in medium bowl. Beat with electric or hand whisk until it turns into a pale mousse with twice the volume.

4. Tip chocolate and flour into mousse. Very gently fold mix together with a large metal spoon, using big light scooping movements to keep the air in. Get right to the bottom of the bowl.

5. Pour mix into ramekins. Sit on baking tray in oven. Cook 12 minutes. Don't open door. You want puds risen, cooked on outside but just soft in the middle.

6. Eat as is. Or run knife round edges, put plate on top, invert. Tap to turn out. Serve it. Awesome.

VARIATION
ORANGE OR LIME
CURD
At STEP 4 add juice of
2 oranges or 4 limes
instead of lemon juice.

Lemon curd butterfly cakes

These are soft, gooey, citrusy. Stick candles in to celebrate
a birthday.

Method

1. Preheat oven to 190°C/375°F/gas 5. Sit paper bun cases in metal bun tin.
2. Slap cake ingredients into large bowl. Beat with electric hand whisk (or
wooden spoon) for 2–3 minutes. You want a soft, pale mix which softly
drops off spoon.
3. Three-quarters fill bun cases. Don't press mix down. Bake 12–15 minutes
or till risen and brown on top, still a bit springy. Cool on rack.
4. Meantime for curd: put butter, sugar, lemon rind and juice to melt in a
bowl sitting over a pan of simmering water. (Bowl must not touch water.)
5. Stir to mix. Tip well-beaten eggs in. Stir until curd thickens to coat back of
wooden spoon. Pour into bowl to cool.
6. Cut centres from top of cold buns. Fill with curd. Chop centres in two.
Sit bits on curd for wings. Dust with icing sugar.

**Makes 12
Cakes**
110 g/4 oz very soft butter
110 g/4 oz caster sugar
110 g/4 oz self-raising
   flour, sifted
1 level tsp baking powder
2 large eggs
Grated rind of 1 lemon
2 drops vanilla essence
1 tbsp orange juice
Icing sugar for dusting

Lemon curd
Use bought lemon curd
or:
Juice and grated rind of
   2 big unwaxed lemons
110 g/4 oz caster sugar
2 very large eggs
50 g/2 oz butter

30 minutes

For 6
Fruit
10 plums poached in
  syrup or 10 ripe fresh
  plums
2 soft bananas, thinly
  sliced
2 ripe nectarines, thinly
  sliced
Few blackberries
Few strawberries
Crumble
100 g/3½ oz plain flour
100 g/3½ oz ground
  almonds
100 g/3½ oz amaretti
  biscuits, crushed
100 g/3½ oz soft butter

Eat with: ice-cream,
crème fraîche, whipped
cream or custard (pg 88).

Amaretti banana soft fruit crumble

Give crumble a crunchy biscuity twist. Sit it on hot soft mixed fruit. (Got any poached plums left over?) Get some melty banana to bring it together.

Method

1. Preheat oven to 200°C/400°F/gas 6.

2. Using fresh plums? Slap them in a pan with water and sugar. Heat to simmer and soften (see page 88) while you make the crumble topping.

3. Using pre-poached plums? Tip straight into shallow ovenproof dish with other fruit to make a single layer. Add syrup to come halfway up fruit.

4. Stick amaretti in freezer bag. Twist top. Bash with rolling pin to crumble (not too small). Tip into bowl with flour, ground almonds, butter cut into bits.

5. Rub mix together by picking it up over the bowl and rubbing lightly and quickly between your fingertips till it looks like biscuity breadcrumbs.

6. Sprinkle crumble evenly over the top of the fruit. Bake for 15 minutes or till it's starting to bubble juices, with the top crisp and golden.

Toffee lemon cream fruit cups

Ideal for a cool pud and a bit of a laugh. Tea cup. Fresh fruit. Lemon cream. Toffee top. Sit cup in a saucer with a spoon and a biscuit.

1. Stick fruit in cups till two-thirds full.
2. Whip cream till just soft. Stir in curd. Cover fruit, almost to the top of the cups. Smooth over. Chill for 20 minutes.

3. Tip sugar into heavy-bottomed pan on gentle heat. Let it melt and bubble till it turns golden brown (no darker – it burns). Pour a thin layer over each cup immediately. Let toffee set for 2 minutes. Crack in there.

For 4
Mix of chopped and whole soft fruit e.g. raspberries, blackberries, strawberries, Chinese gooseberries, peaches, nectarines, banana, grapes, diced fresh mango soaked in lime juice
Double or whipping cream
2 tbsps lemon curd to taste (page 117)

Topping
110 g/4 oz caster sugar

Ginger brandy snap baskets

Snappy, wacky-shaped crisp ginger baskets to fill with berries or whatever fruit's about. Suits ice-cream, sliced banana and a chocolate sauce. Note: make flat snaps if you like for ice-cream sandwiches. Or curl big ones for stuffing or dipping in chocolate.

Method

1. Preheat oven to 160°C/325°F/gas 3.
2. Slap sugar, butter and syrup into a saucepan. Heat gently to melt.
3. Stir to mix. Remove from heat. Sift flour and ginger into pan. Add juice. Beat well with a wooden spoon. Leave to cool for a few minutes.
4. Line a baking tray with silicone paper or butter it really well. Drop dessert or tablespoons of the mix onto it, well apart. They grow 4–5 inches. Bake for 8 minutes or till lacy and golden. Watch them!
5. Remove. Leave to cool for 1–2 minutes till you can lift them off with a spatula. Gently press snaps over moulds (upturned jars or sauce bottles) while soft. Leave to cool for 2 minutes. PS For curls, roll mix round wooden spoon handle and leave or curl and press with your fingers.

For 6
50 g/2 oz granulated sugar
50 g/2 oz butter
2 tbsps golden syrup
50 g/2 oz plain white flour
1 level tsp ground ginger
2 tsps lemon juice

leftovers

Work the system. Cook and enjoy these great roasts with all the extras when you've tons of time. Enjoy what's left when you're in a hurry. Key note for cooks: these guys may have longer cooking times, but the prepping's speedier than in loads of speedy cooking.

Roast beef

Get rib on the bone for a sweet meat. Boned joints like sirloin or rib eye are cool. Not sure what you want? Ask a butcher. Chuck spuds round joint for best roasties.

FOR 6
1.8 kg/4 lb beef rib on bone or
**   1.35 kg/3 lb boned rib joint**
2 tbsps olive oil
Salt and pepper

Method

1. Get beef out of fridge 1–2 hours before cooking. Weigh it and calculate cooking time (see guide).
2. Preheat oven to 230°C/450°F/gas 8. Sit beef in roasting tin. Run sharp knife lengthways down fat to score lightly. Season. Rub oil into fat.
3. Cook beef for 15 minute hot blast. Reduce to 180°C/350°F/gas 4 for rest of cooking time. Spoon juices over a boneless joint a few times. Joints on the bone take care

of themselves. Test for doneness with skewer. Medium rare (pink and tender inside, seared brown outside) is cool.
4. Remove beef. Set to rest in a warm place for 15 minutes while you crisp spuds and add water to juices to simmer for great gravy.

Cooking times:
Use your eye. (I do.) But rough guide: 15 minute blast then:
On bone joint: 12 minutes per pound (rare), 15 per pound (medium), 20 (well done).
Boned joint: 10 minutes per pound (rare), 12 per pound (medium), 15 (well done).

Roast orange mustard glazed gammon

Lovin' it hot with veg. Cold with scrambled or poached eggs. Chop into stir-fry, crêpes, pastas, salads. Top sandwich.

FOR 6
2 kg/4½ lbs gammon or bacon
**   joint**
Water to cover

300 ml/10 fl oz orange or apple
   juice or cider, plus a little extra
1 onion, peeled

Glaze:
1 tbsp made English mustard
1 tbsp chunky marmalade
1 tbsp runny honey
1 tbsp soft brown sugar
15 whole cloves

Method
1. Day before: Sit meat to cover in
large bowl cold water in fridge to
get excess salt out.
2. On the day: Drain meat. Put it in
pan with juice or cider. Just cover
with water. Add onion.
3. Boil gently for 1 hour. Meantime
mix glaze ingredients (not cloves).
4. Preheat oven to 200°C/400°F/
gas 6. Drain meat over bowl. Save
stock for soup if not too salty.

5. Cut skin from ham leaving fat
exposed. Cut across in diamond
pattern with sharp knife.
6. Stud with cloves. Put ham in
baking dish with little extra juice or
cider. Smear two-thirds of glaze over.
7. Cook 45 minutes. Brush with
remaining glaze a few times.

Simple brilliant roast chicken
Roast. Eat. Repeat for salad
bowls and plates. Sandwiches,
wraps and stacks. Stuffing for
Tex-Mex and crêpes. Chucking
in stir-fries.

FOR 4–6
1 large good quality chicken
Few slices bacon, pancetta,
   Parma ham to cover top
1 lemon
Any herbs (optional)
Salt and pepper

Olive oil and bit of butter

Method
1. Preheat oven to 190°C/375°F/
gas 5.
2. Sit chicken in roasting tin. Grind
black pepper over it. Lay bacon
over breast to keep meat moist.
3. Slip 2 lemon chunks inside bird
to moisten and flavour.
4. Drizzle oil over bird with bit in tin.
5. Roast for 20 mins per 450 g/1 lb
weight plus additional 20 minutes.
That's it!
6. Test for doneness. Stick skewer
or sharp knife into bird. Juices
should run clear, meat white. Rest
for 10 minutes. Gravy? Mix with
water, wine. Bubble it up and
pour it.

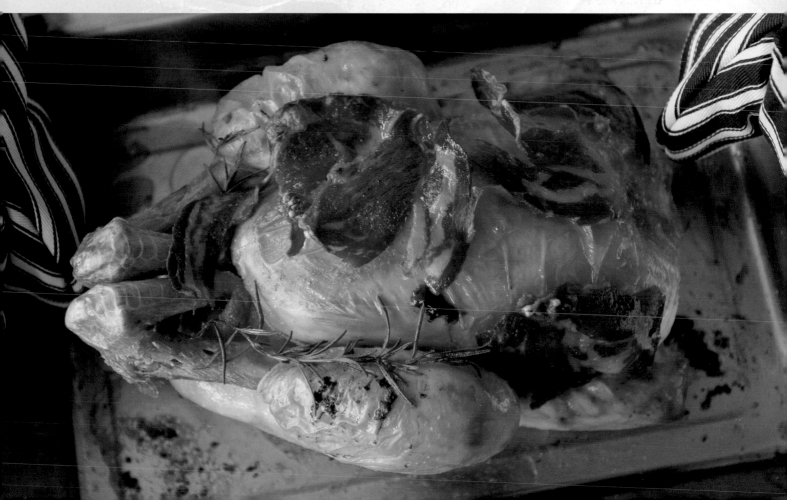

essential extras

Extras give good food that cheeky edge (bit like the movies – wouldn't work without them). Get these hanging out in your fridge, cupboard, breadbin.

DRESSINGS
Eating equivalent of cool accessories. Any salad's naked without one.

My sparky dressing
The one for me. I love balsamic.

Good pinch of caster sugar
Pinch of salt
1 tbsp balsamic vinegar
4–6 tbsps extra virgin olive oil

Method
1. Stick sugar, salt, balsamic in bowl.
2. Whisk together. Add oil bit by bit.
3. Taste and adjust. Or stick the lot in a jar. Put the top on. Shake it.

Mum's mustard one
Complex flavour. Good and punchy.

2 tsps mustard (English, Dijon or wholegrain)
1 tsp honey or caster sugar
1 garlic clove, crushed, or a little chopped shallot (optional)
2 tbsps lemon juice or any wine vinegar
6 tbsps extra virgin olive oil (sub in a little walnut oil if you like)
Salt and black pepper

Method
1. Mix mustard, honey or sugar, seasoning, wine vinegar or lemon juice in a bowl.
2. Add garlic or shallot, if using. Beat oil in. Or shake in a jar till it emulsifies.

STOCKS
You'll be needing these for soups and risottos.

Chicken stock
Go freestyle with your veg...

1 roast chicken carcass
1 onion, peeled and quartered
1 stick celery
1 carrot
Any herbs
3.4 litres/6 pints water

Method
1. Throw everything into a large pan with any extra gravy and jelly.
2. Boil. Skim off any scum. Simmer very gently for 2 hours.
3. Strain in colander over bowl. Cool then cover. Chill or freeze.

Vegetable stock
For meat-free soups and risottos.

2 large onions
1 stick celery
2 leeks
3 carrots
Few black peppercorns
Any herbs
2 cloves garlic
Good pinch of salt
Juice of 1 lemon
2.3 litres/4 pints water

Method
1. Wash and roughly chop all veg.
2. Chuck into pan with water, lemon, seasoning.
3. Boil up. Simmer 1–2 hours. Strain though sieve.

Cheesy option

Lovely. Works well on crisp lettuce, rocket, chopped chicory.

4 tbsps extra virgin olive oil
Juice of 1 lemon
2 tbsps freshly grated Parmesan
Salt and black pepper

Method

Chuck it in a bowl. Whisk it together.

Homemade mayo

Make the basic then go with the options. A great dip with veg sticks. Mix to music.

2 egg yolks
½ tsp each of salt, dry mustard
    and caster sugar
250 ml/8 fl oz sunflower or
    groundnut oil
50ml/2 fl oz olive oil
2 tbsps lemon juice or white
    wine vinegar
1 tbsp hot water

Method

1. Beat yolks, salt, mustard, sugar in a large bowl with balloon whisk. (Sit bowl on tea towel to stop it slipping.)
2. Mix oils in a jug. Pour the oil, drip by drip, onto the eggs, whisking all the time. Keep it slow to start so mix won't curdle. Let it thicken.
3. When you've used half the oil, stop. Stir in half the juice or vinegar.
4. Pour remaining oil in a very slow trickle. Keep whisking.
5. Pour in remaining oil in a slow trickle. Keep whisking. Add rest of juice or vinegar and water.
6. Taste. Adjust seasoning. Keeps for a week in an airtight container in the fridge.

Variations

Garlic mayo (aioli) At step 1 add 2–3 fat cloves of crushed garlic to the basic ingredients.

Dill and mustard (for swift fish) Add 2 teaspoons of sugar and 2 tablespoons Dijon mustard with the egg yolks. Use 150 ml/5 fl oz sunflower oil. When mixed, stir in 1–2 tablespoons fresh chopped dill.

Hot mayo Add 2 tablespoons wasabi or harissa paste to the eggs instead of mustard.

SPREADS
Smashed bean mix

Tex-Mex needs own re-fries. Up the quantities for parties.

1 medium onion, finely chopped
1 clove garlic, crushed
1 tbsp olive oil
1 x 440 g/14 oz can red kidney
    beans
Pinch cumin (optional)
Pinch dried oregano (optional)
Pinch sugar
2 tsps white wine vinegar

Method

1. Fry onion and garlic in oil for 4 minutes or till soft.
2. Meantime, drain and rinse beans well.
3. Slap beans and optional spices in with onion.
4. Fry till beans start to get mushy.
5. Add vinegar to taste. Leave beans crushed or mash completely if you want.

Tapenade

A great olive pâté. Spread on toast, bruschetta, fish. Stir into pasta. Veggies – skip the anchovies.

110 g/4 oz pitted black olives
1 tbsp capers, rinsed
1 fat clove garlic
4 anchovy fillets, drained
    (optional)
1 tsp Dijon mustard
Good squeeze lemon juice
Black pepper
4 tbsps extra virgin olive oil

Method

Chuck everything but oil into processor. Blitz. Trickle oil into mix through funnel while still blitzing for a thickish paste. It lasts, but fridge it.

Pesto

Stir into pasta or rice. Drizzle over fish, lamb or griddled veg. Get a herb plot sorted.

110 g/4 oz fresh basil leaves
150 ml/5 fl oz olive oil
25 g/1 oz pine nuts (optional)
2 plump cloves garlic
50 g/2 oz Parmesan, grated

Method

1. Blitz everything but cheese in processor.
2. Stir cheese in. Chill it.

Variation

Use coriander or rocket instead of basil.

Apple chutney

Save time. Here's a year's worth. Goes with new-style deli meats, cheeses, ham, gammon, salads, even guacamole!

MAKES 4 x 900 g/2 lb jars
2 kg/4½ lbs cooking or firm eating apples
600 ml/1 pint malt vinegar
6 fat cloves garlic
675 g/1½ lbs soft dark brown sugar
125 g/4½ oz stoned dates, chopped
4 tsps ground ginger
2 tsps ground mixed spice
1 tsp cayenne pepper
1 tsp salt

Method

1. Peel, core, chop apples. Tip into large heavy-based saucepan.
2. Add garlic and half vinegar. Cook on gentle heat, stirring with wooden spoon, till mix is just pulpy.
3. Add rest of vinegar, sugar, dates, salt, spices.
4. Cook gently for 30 minutes, stirring so it doesn't stick. Mix needs to be thick with the odd lump.
5. Meantime wash jars and dry in oven at 140°C/275°F/gas 1.
6. Ladle hot chutney into jars. Top chutney with a wax disc from a jam kit to cover.
7. Dampen cellophane disc to cover each pot. Secure with elastic band. When jars are cold, label and store in dark place. Leave to mature for 2 months. Get eating it.

Chicken liver pâté

Top family eat. Lasts a week.

FOR 8
400 g/14 oz pack chicken livers (defrosted if frozen)
Bit of milk to cover
50 g/2 oz butter plus 2–3 tbsps for sealing pot
3 fat shallots, chopped
3 cloves garlic, crushed
3–4 rashers rindless bacon
2–3 sprigs thyme leaves
Slug brandy, sherry or apple juice
175 g/6 oz light cream or curd cheese
1 lemon
Salt and black pepper

Method

1. Soak livers in a bit of milk for 20 minutes. Drain and chop them.
2. Melt butter in pan. Add shallot and garlic. Fry gently for 3 minutes. Add chopped bacon.
3. Fry 5 minutes. Add liver. Cook, turning till browned outside, still pink inside.
4. Turn up heat. Whack in brandy, sherry or juice. Let it sizzle for 2

minutes. Add herbs, black pepper, little salt.
5. Tip mix into processor. Add cheese, lots of lemon juice. Blitz. Taste. Adjust seasoning.
6. Spoon into bowl. Cool for 5 minutes. Cover with melted butter. Chill. Best after a day.

BREADS

The great white loaf

Own bread? Cool. Can't better it.

FOR a 900 g/2 lb loaf
700 g/1½ lb strong white flour
2 tsps salt
Good pinch of sugar
15 g/½ oz butter
1 x 7 g sachet easy-blend yeast
425 ml/15 fl oz warm water
Butter for greasing tin

7. Slap back on board to knead for 2 minutes.

8. Shape dough into loaf as long as a 900 g/2 lb tin, three times the width. Turn the outer thirds in under central one so it fits greased tin. Put it in.

9. Leave under carrier in warm place till risen higher than top of tin. Meanwhile preheat oven to 230°C/450°F/gas 8.

10. Bake 30 minutes. Turn out. Tap bottom – should sound hollow. Sit, tinless, back in oven for 5–10 minutes if you need. Cool on rack.

Top treacle bread
Speedy, tasty family favourite.

FOR 2 x 900 g/2 lb loaves
2 tbsps black treacle
Up to 850 ml/1½ pints warm water
50 g/2 oz fresh yeast
450 g/1 lb strong white flour
450g/1 lb strong wholemeal flour
1 tsp salt

1. Preheat oven to 200°C/400°F/gas 6. Grease two 900 g/2 lb loaf tins well inside and up over top edges.

2. Mix treacle with 150 ml/5 fl oz water and crumbled yeast. Cover with tea towel and leave till frothy. Then add remaining water.

3. Sift flour into big bowl with salt. Gradually add liquid, mixing with wooden spoon till you get a soft dough that's not sloppy.

4. Spoon mix equally between tins. Sit a carrier bag over each tin like a large hat to keep it warm. Sit in warm place till dough rises above the top of the tin – not spilling over!

5. Slap in oven for 30 minutes. Turn out to check for doneness. Knock

on bottom of loaf. It should sound hollow and feel hard. Sit it upside-down in oven for a few more minutes if it needs.

6. Cool on rack. Makes fab toast. Great taste with sweet and savoury.

Fast scone bread
Eat the day you make with soup; butter it, ham, jam and cheese it.

FOR 1 loaf
375 g/13 oz self-raising flour
1½ tsps salt
90 g/3¼ oz butter, melted
125 ml/4 fl oz milk
125 ml/4 fl oz water
Milk to brush it
Flour to dust it

Method
1. Preheat oven to 220°C/425°F/gas 7.

2. Hold sieve well above large bowl. Sift flour and salt.

3. Make dent in flour. Tip butter, milk, water into it. Mix with fork till it makes a dough. Pull lightly together.

4. Sit dough on lightly floured board. Knead lightly for a few seconds till just smooth. Shape into a 6-inch round. Put on greased tray.

5. Make six half-inch cuts into loaf as if dividing a pizza. Brush with little milk.

6. Sprinkle bit of flour over it. Cook for 10 minutes. Set timer. Drop temperature to 180°C/350°F/gas 4. Cool on rack.

Variations
Cheese and onion
At STEP 3 chuck in a bit of grated Cheddar, bit of mustard powder, sliced spring onion.

Fruit
At STEP 3 chuck in 1 tablespoon caster sugar and a handful of sultanas or other dried fruit.

Method
1. Chuck sifted flour, salt and sugar in big bowl.

2. Drop butter in. Rub it into flour with your fingers till it's invisible. Add yeast.

3. Mix water in gradually with wooden spoon.

4. Use your hands to pull into soft, firm dough with bit more water if needed.

5. Slap dough on floured board to knead, i.e. punch, stretch and work out on it for 10 minutes or slap into mixer bowl with dough hook and let it do the work.

6. Tip elastic smooth dough into bowl. Pop carrier bag over bowl like egg cosy. Leave in warm place till doubles in volume (1–2 hours depending on temperature).

index

index

mozzarella in carrozza **35**
mushrooms: lettuce wrapped lamb'n'mushroom stir-fry **87**; mushroom, rocket & balsamic sandwich **29**; mushroom crêpe roll **113**; mushroom risotto **104**; mushroom tart **95**; potato, pea & mushroom curry **115**
mustard dressing **122**

N nectarines: fruit in a paper parcel **48**
noodles: noodle cake **65**; noodle soup **64**; stir-fry noodles & beansprouts **65**

O omelettes: in baguette **45**; chorizo **45**; dippers **47**; flat fried with potato & courgette **47**; flip top, stir-fry **44**; pizza-style **46**
orange almond neat biscuits **89**
oranges: honey orange biscuit crunch yogurt combo **17**; orange boost smoothie **19**; tropic smoothie **19**

P pak choi: stir-fried greens **63**; noodle soup **64**
pancakes: raspberry ginger cream **71** see also **crêpes**
Parma ham: Parma ham & melon **12**; Parma ham & mozzarella plate **12**; Sam's special club sandwich **29**; tomozzarella stacks **83**
pasta dishes: camping pasta with tomato or tuna'n'tomato sauce **79**; courgette herb cream pasta **81**; hot penne with cool tomatoes & olives **67**; pasta with tomato sauce & pesto **66**; sausage & mustard creamy pasta **81**; spaghetti Bolognese **80**
pâtés: chicken liver **124**; guacamole **38**; smoked fish **38**; spicy hummus **37**; tapenade **123**;
peaches: fruit in a paper parcel **48**
peanut butter & banana toast **21**
pear & avocado combo **15**
potato, pea & mushroom curry **115**
penne with cool tomatoes & olives **67**
pesto **124**
pineapples: tropic smoothie **19**
pitta bread: chunky guacamole & garlic **38**; Greek salad pitta **25**; sizzling spuds & stuff **26** see also **tortillas** and **wraps**
pizza cheese on baked baguette **33**
pizza-style omelette **46**
pizzas: basic pizza dough **96**; cool tomato **97**; deep lush baked one **97**; Margherita **97**; thin, crispy griddled one **97**; toppings **97**
plums: amaretti banana soft fruit crumble **118**; bedhead Turkish Delight plums **88**; fruit in a paper parcel **48**
pork burger **76**
potatoes: baby **62**; cheese'n'onion mash **85**; flat fried omelette with potato & courgette **47**; garlic mash **111**; hot potato salad with chorizo **62**; potato, pea & mushroom curry **115**; smooth everyday mash **84**; speedy fried **61**;

sizzling spuds & stuff in pitta **26**; sweet potato mash **85**
prawns: prawn & chicken stir-fry **86**; prawn plate **14**
puddings: amaretti banana soft fruit crumble **118**; chocolate puds **116**; Eton blueberry mess **70**; ginger brandy snap baskets **119**; lemon curd butterfly cakes **117**; toffee lemon cream fruit cups **119**

Q quesadillas **103**

R rabbit (cheese) on toast **32**
raita **36**
raspberries: berry yogurt crunch **17**; blackberry smoothie **18**; breakfast boost smoothie **18**; exotic banana smoothie **18**; fruit in a paper parcel **48**; raspberry ginger cream pancakes **71** refried beans: quesadillas **103**; smashed bean mix **123**
risottos: mushroom **104**; salmon, cheese & green leaf **105**
roast beef **120**
roast beef plate **13**
roast chicken **121**
roast chicken plate **13**
roast gammon: honey & marmalade gammon plate **13**; roast orange mustard glazed gammon **120–1**

S salads: all day breakfast **43**; Caesar **40**; chicken tonnato **41**; couscous **69**; curried chicken waldorf **41**; Greek salad pitta **25**; hot potato salad with chorizo **62**; sizzled halloumi & green leaves **42**; tuna & beanie **39**
salmon: basic fillets **56**; cajun spiced **57**; fishcakes **107**; griddled fish chunks **57**; salmon, cheese & green leaf risotto **105**; smoked salmon plate **14**
salsa verde **55**
Sam's special club sandwich **29**
sandwiches: club **27–9**; egg & mozzarella open **30**; fish kebab **31**; ham, egg mayo & chilli jam **24**; mushroom, rocket & balsamic **29**; speedy steak **30** see also **bread combos**, **wraps** and **pittas**
sauces: barbecue **98**; Bolognese **80**; custard **88**; ginger teriyaki drizzle **53**; harissa dressing **68**; jammy **111**; salsa verde **55**; sweet & sour red jelly **54**; tomato **66**, **79**; tuna'n'tomato **79** see also **dressings**
sausages: cassoulet **108**; sausage & mustard creamy pasta **81**; trekking breakfast **78**
scone bread **125**
scrambled egg on toast with asparagus & balsamic **36**
shakes **19**
smoothies **18–19**

soufflés: easy cheese **109**
soups: cheese & watercress **93**; noodle **64**; tomato & lentil **92**
spaghetti Bolognese **80**
spreads: pesto **124**; smashed bean mix **123**; tapenade **123**
steaks: brilliant basic **52**; chilli spice mustard beefsteak **53**; ginger teriyaki drizzle **53**; with lemon, parsley & garlic rub **53**; peppered **53**; steak sandwich **30**
stir-fries: flip top omelette **44**; greens **63**; lamb'n'mushroom **87**; noodles & beansprouts **65**
stocks **122**
strawberries: berry yogurt crunch **17**; fruit in a paper parcel **48**; strawberry lite smoothie **18**
sweet & sour red jelly sauce **54**
sweet potato mash **85**

T tabbouleh **69**
tapenade **123**
Tex-Mex dishes **100–3**
tikka masala dhal, fast **115**
toasts **20– 1**; melba toast **38**
toffee lemon cream fruit cups **119**
tofu: noodle soup **64**
tomatoes: auberfeta stacks **83**; camping pasta with tomato or tuna'n'tomato sauce **79**; hot penne with cool tomatoes & olives **67**; hot tomatoes **62**; pizza toppings **97**; tomato & garlic toast **20**; tomato & lentil soup **92**; tomato sauce **66**, **79**; tomato tart **95**; tomozzarella stacks **83**
tortillas **100–3** see also **wraps** and **pittas**
tostadas **101**
treacle bread **125**
trekking breakfast **78**
trout: smoked fish pâté **38**; speedy baked trout **58**
tuna: brilliant basic steak **56**; camping pasta with tuna'n'tomato sauce **79**; fish kebab sandwich **31**; griddled fish chunks **57**; tuna, spring onion & cucumber wrap **25**; tuna & beanie salad **39**; tuna melt **35**; tuna with ginger lime fish drizzle **57**

V vegetable dishes: great griddled veg **60**; green beans with tomato & garlic **61**; stir-fried greens **63**; hot potato salad with chorizo **62**; hot tomatoes **62**; speedy fried potatoes **61**
vegetable stock **122**

W watercress & cheese soup **93**
wraps: huevos rancheros **82**; tuna, spring onion & cucumber **25** see also **pittas** and **tortillas**

Y yogurt and fruit combos **17**
Yorkshire fried fish **59**

127

shopping list

Stock up with stuff and you're up and running… Every fast cook needs stuff to cook with. Here's my list of basics. Maybe you've got a load of it. If not, don't rush out and get it in one. Build your stock as you work through the recipes.

Bottles & jars of stuff
Good olive oil (for cooking)
Extra virgin olive oil (for salads)
Sunflower oil
Sesame oil (for stir-fries)
Groundnut oil (for curries)
White wine vinegar
Rice wine vinegar
Rice wine
Good balsamic vinegar
Soy sauce
Oyster sauce
Fish sauce
Tomato ketchup
Worcestershire sauce
Tomato purée
Passata or sugocasa
Runny honey
Maple syrup
Cherry jam
Redcurrant jelly
Veggie stock powder (I use Marigold)
English made mustard
Dijon mustard
Black olives

Capers
Mayonnaise
Harissa paste
Curry paste
Mango chutney
Jalapeno pickles

Packets
Dried yeast
English mustard powder
Basmati rice (for stir-fries and other dishes)
Arborio and vialone nano rice (for risottos)
Couscous
Bulgar wheat
Red lentils
Pasta – linguine, penne, spaghetti, tagliatelle
Semolina
Dried egg noodles
Plain white flour
Strong white breadflour (for pizza)
Caster sugar
Soft brown sugar
Creamed coconut

Tins & things
Chopped tomatoes
Chickpeas
Mushy peas
Baked beans
Red kidney beans
Re-fried beans
Dolphin-friendly tuna
Black treacle
Golden syrup

Spices & flavourings
Sea salt
Fine salt
Black peppercorns
Cracked black peppercorns
Dried chillies
Vanilla extract
Oregano
Chinese five spice powder
Smoked paprika
Turmeric
Cinnamon sticks
Cumin seeds
Mustard seeds
Poppy seeds

Chilli powder
Rosewater
Garam masala
Cardamom pods
Powdered ginger
Dried cumin

Dairy
Butter
Eggs
Parmesan cheese
Strong Cheddar cheese
Gruyère cheese
Feta cheese
Halloumi cheese

I always have loadsa lemons, limes, fresh ginger, garlic, shallots, and fresh herbs like parsley, coriander, basil and dill too.

Thanks to all my brilliant mates for helping out with this book…
Nick Howard, Tom Yule, Joe Coulter, Jess Taylor, Charlotte Parkinson, Olivia Towers, Verity Myers, Henry Preen, Dom Hanley, Hannah Jackson, Hattie Coulter, Alex Crossley, Robert Kinnell, Will Butterworth, Anton Holness and Kamal Sharma.

Ta to Sarah Coggles Clothing, Next Generation Gym, Scott's butchers, Henshelwood's Deli, and Octavio and Heidi's Bottega della Langhe for letting us take photographs and for selling lovely stuff. Big thanks to Louise Rooke, champion food tester.

Respect to Lorne and his camera. Denise, Louise and Ellen from Walker for all their support.

Finally, love and thanks to my lovely family, that's Polly, Tom, KR and Alice. Special love and thanks to Dad for the washing-up and for coming through it all.

First published 2006 by Walker Books Ltd
87 Vauxhall Walk, London SE11 5HJ

10 9 8 7 6 5 4 3 2 1

© 2006 Sam Stern and Susan Stern

Photographs by Lorne Campbell

The moral rights of the authors have been asserted

British Library Cataloguing in Publication Data:
a catalogue record for this book is available from the British Library

ISBN-13: 978-1-4063-0249-3
ISBN-10: 1-4063-0249-X

www.walkerbooks.co.uk